COLD TRAIL

OTHER FIVE STAR TITLES BY CLIFF FARRELL:

Desperate Journey
The White Feather

COLD TRAIL

A WESTERN DUO

CLIFF FARRELL

FIVE STAR

An imprint of Thomson Gale, a part of The Thomson Corporation

Detroit • New York • San Francisco • New Haven, Conn. • Waterville, Maine • London

Copyright © 2006 by Mildred Hueg.
"Stampede in Avalanche Pass" first appeared in *Dime Western* (5/34). Copyright © 1934 by Popular Publications, Inc. Copyright © renewed 1962 by Cliff Farrell. Copyright © 2006 by Mildred Hueg for restored material.
"Cold Trail" first appeared under the title "End of Steel" in the *Toronto Star Weekly* (8/10/57). Copyright © 1957 by Cliff Farrell. Copyright © renewed 1985 by Mildred Farrell. Copyright © 2006 by Mildred Hueg for restored material.
Thomson Gale is part of The Thomson Corporation.
Thomson and Star Logo and Five Star are trademarks and Gale is a registered trademark used herein under license.

Set in 11 pt. Plantin.

LIBRARY OF CONGRESS CATALOGING-IN-PUBLICATION DATA

Farrell, Cliff.
    [Stampede in Avalanche Pass]
    Cold trail : a western duo / by Cliff Farrell. — 1st ed.
      p. cm.
    ISBN 1-59414-410-9 (alk. paper)
    I. Farrell, Cliff. Cold trail. II. Title.
    PS3556.A766S73 2006
    813'.54—dc22
                                             2006023180

U.S. Hardcover:
ISBN 13: 978-1-59414-410-3
ISBN 10: 1-59414-410-9

First Edition. First Printing: November 2006.

Published in 2006 in conjunction with Golden West Literary Agency.

Printed in the United States of America on permanent paper
10 9 8 7 6 5 4 3 2 1

CONTENTS

★ ★ ★ ★ ★

STAMPEDE IN AVALANCHE PASS

★ ★ ★ ★ ★

I

For the last mile Del Halliday had been paying less and less attention to the incessant flow of conversation of Foghorn Peters, his burly foreman. Also, Del was no longer plucking and chewing the tall straws of the foxtail grass that dotted the slant—a habit of Del's when all things were going well. They had been inspecting the winter range on the high benches of Del's Rolling H Ranch all morning, and were returning to the valley, well pleased with what they had seen. This September the thick, brown mountain grama lay cured on the stalk like a carpet; it would soon be needed beyond the fence that had barred the stock from the high range all summer.

But now Del was rising uneasily in his stirrups, to sweep the valley with restless, gray eyes. He could see his spread, nestling along the cottonwood-bordered creek three miles away, and he had a clear view to the rims of the low Lost Creek Hills that enclosed the valley to the east. He hipped about and stared with growing concern southward to where Lost Creek Valley narrowed into a bottleneck notch.

The tiny lines about Del's keen eyes deepened and his mouth was thinned out. Del was flat-shouldered and taller than he seemed at first glance. He was leathery brown, and had a rugged, fighting chin. What Del had, he had fought for. He had fought to keep the Rolling H, had fought harder to keep it growing each year. He had been a slim, drawling, grinning, gangling young cowpuncher when he began it. He was like a blade of tempered steel now.

"You've got the world by the tail with a downhill pull, Del." Foghorn was booming along in a voice like distant thunder. "I been ridin' fer forty years, man an' boy, an' I never seen grass to beat that on the benches. The brand shore will fatten up on that winter range. You'll . . . say, what's wrong?"

Del had suddenly lifted his horse out of its lazy dog trot.

"Plenty," Del snapped over his shoulder. "Reef that cayuse, Foghorn, an' save your breath for hard work. I knew things had been runnin' too smooth the last six months. You've been chewin' the fat too hard to notice the scarcity of cattle here, where there ought to be scads of 'em. But look down there at the end of the valley."

Foghorn rose in his stirrups, too, shading his eyes to peer ahead. There the valley sloped gently for two miles to the bottleneck through which the yellowish, dead face of the desert frowned. Deadhorse Sink lay in the notch.

As they hurled their horses on at breakneck speed, Del gritted: "If they've broke through the sink fence, we're in for some tough work!" As they came within a mile, Del gave a groan. "There's a break in the fence!" he cried bitterly. "A lot of 'em have drifted through already."

"How could they have busted that fence?" Foghorn rumbled. "We built it triple-strong, an' I rode it only two days ago."

Del was peering ahead grimly. Cattle were thick in the vicinity of the two-mile barrier of wire that stretched from rim to rim of the steep-walled bottleneck, although grazing was poor on the valley side of the fence.

"They didn't bust it," Del said, his words clipped and tense. "That fence has been cut by some treacherous skunk in half a dozen places. A couple hundred head are in the sink already."

Foghorn could see the openings in the wire now. More steers were grazing through, lured by the scent of lush, wet marsh grass. But they were being tempted to their doom. It was here that Lost Creek sank into the earth again, and the place of its disappearance was a mile-long marsh that was a death trap.

"Some damned sheep-walkin' skunk done it!" Foghorn bellowed.

"That goes double for me, too," Del rejoined. "We'll haze all the critters out that ain't bogged down. Then we'll splice up the holes. You'll fog back to the ranch an' bring Bill an' Gus. We'll need plenty of rope, too. Hear 'em bawlin'! There must be a couple score of the poor critters so far out we can't see 'em. They've sunk down below the brush. I'll start draggin' 'em out, while you bring the boys. . . ."

II

As the sun touched the rim of the mighty Bluestones to the west, the job was done. Four exhausted, mud-plastered men dismounted and looked at each other. The crickets and toads in the swamp were starting their dismal death dirge to the steers that had been swallowed beneath the quivering surface.

"Forty at least," Del estimated wearily. "Well, that won't ruin us by a long shot. But if we hadn't discovered it when we did. . . ."

They all knew that the Rolling H had narrowly escaped disaster.

"A man that would do a sneakin' thing like that would hide a calf from its maw," Foghorn boomed.

Del collected a spat of mud from his chaps and flicked it away. "It wasn't a lone-handed job," he remarked tersely. His three riders looked at him in surprise. "You rannies don't think the stock all wandered down here of their own will, do you? They were shoved down to this end of the valley. It must have been done last night. It was full moon. One man couldn't have

11

turned the trick. It took a full crew, take it from me, *amigos.*"

"Wal, consarn me for a sand flea!" Foghorn bellowed. "What was the grand idea?"

"If I knew what the idea was, I'd know who pulled it," Del said, turning to mount. "An' if I knew that, I'd try to take somebody apart an see what makes 'em tick."

Then he paused and waited. Distant hoof beats sounded. Soon, seven riders emerged from the brush of the creek to the north, and came swinging up rapidly.

"Howdy, Halliday," a twanging voice sounded.

Del recognized Spot Sherill, the sharp-chinned owner of the big Double S Circle, which occupied the range beyond the hills to the east. Sherill, middle-aged and turkey-necked, carried a reputation as a hard businessman who never made a mistake. But he had erred when he sold Lost Creek Valley to Del five years previously.

Sherill had believed the valley was worthless. Except for a mere trickle in early spring, Lost Creek had never carried enough water to support cattle. It had never occurred to Sherill that it was an underground stream. But Del Halliday's roving gray eyes had guessed that fact, and Del's bronzed hands had placed the few shots of dynamite that had brought the full flow of the stream to the surface at the north end of the valley. It was a perpetual stream now, and it had made the valley the best cattle range in the Bluestone country.

Del, his hands on his hips, eyed Sherill's six companions. They were strangers; garbed as cowpunchers, they did not fit the rôle. One, who was amazingly broad and squatty of figure, packed a brace of .45s. The others carried rifles and six-shooters.

Foghorn leaned close to Del and with an effort toned his whisper down to a mere murmur. "That *hombre* who looks like a toad is an old-time gunslinger . . . Frog Durkin, from the

Panhandle. Plenty poisonous."

The seven newcomers dismounted, and crowded close about the four Rolling H men. Del became watchful. There was something off-color about all this.

"I heard you was havin' some grief . . . ," Sherill began.

"Is that why you're grinnin'?" Del said tersely. "How did you hear about it?"

"I didn't," Sherill said easily. "We seen you boys snakin' 'em out of the sink as we come over the hills. I was aimin' on callin' on you, Halliday. I got some business to talk over."

"You brought along a lot of witnesses," Del said pointedly. "Go ahead, spit it out, Sherill."

"Here?" Sherill said, trying to look surprised.

"As good a place as any," Del observed. He was not picking a quarrel, but at the moment he was not going far to avoid one, either. From the moment he saw Sherill's approach, Del had been sure he knew who had sent his cattle into the sink.

Sherill rubbed his jaw with a bony hand. "It's this way, Halliday. I've decided to buy you out."

"That's nice."

"Yeah, I need more range. I only sold you this valley because you was a young feller that needed a little help."

"How much?" Del shot back.

Sherill considered. "Oh, I'll give you eight thousand for the valley. I don't want your cattle."

"That's just what I paid you for it," Del remarked with a calmness that even surprised himself. He wanted to roar out an angry opinion of such a measly price. The valley was worth triple that sum.

"Land is cheap now," Sherill said smoothly. "An' then I don't reckon that you're ever goin' to make much money raisin' cows in Lost Creek Valley. Do you, Durkin?"

This last was addressed at the bulky gunman. "No, I don't

reckon you'll ever get very far in this valley, young feller," Durkin said, rousing himself from his heavy silence. "It don't look so healthy here for some folks."

Del drew his tobacco sack from his shirt pocket with steady hands. Foghorn, who had seen Del in action in the past, could detect the little white line along Del's jaw bone, a warning that the young rancher was gathering himself for something. But the odds against them were fearfully heavy. Only Del and Foghorn were armed, and they packed only a six-shooter each. Bill Andrews and Gus Little had not delayed their start from the ranch to get their guns.

"I savvy," Del said, extracting a paper and making a spill of it. "If I don't sell out to you, there'll be more of my fences cut, an' a lot of other cute little tricks like that."

"You got my offer," Sherill said. He was sure of himself, and did not even deny it. "Take it before I change my mind an' cut the price. What's your answer, Halliday?"

Del squeezed the half-filled sack absently and shook it to loosen the tobacco. Then with a quick flirt of his arm he sent a shower of the gritty, dry stuff into the faces of Durkin and his five gunmen. They staggered back with oaths, their hands flashing to their holsters. But the stinging tobacco had worked into their eyes, and in the second or two needed to clear their vision they were covered by Del and Foghorn.

"There's your answer," Del gritted. "Jerk your paws away from that gun, Durkin, or you'll get worse than tobacco."

Sherill and his gunmen were lifting their arms, crestfallen.

"Gus, you an' Bill throw Sherill into the sink," Del said. "He'll feel at home wallerin' in the mud. But first, you better take their hardware."

Sherill cursed, loud and long, as the brawny cowpunchers advanced on him. "Don't you . . ."

But they seized him, tossed him over the fence, caught him

again before he could scuttle away, and heaved him ten feet into the oozy muck. He gave a howl of terror and floundered back to firmer footing.

"Now take your boss, an' shuck out of here, Durkin," Dell said to the gunman. "If I ever see you in this valley again, one of us will go under."

Spot Sherill came, bedraggled and slinking, back to his horse. The seven raging men rode away into the gathering darkness.

Del stood a moment, his gray eyes brooding. There was no triumph in his face, although his riders were whacking each other's backs. "What'll they try next?" he muttered.

"They can't do anything," Foghorn declared. "We'll ride fence every day, till Sherill gets tired of payin' his gunslingers."

"Yeah, an' we'll ride fence at night, too," Del said. "You're slated for the first trick with me tonight, Foghorn."

III

Del and Foghorn spent a weary, monotonous night. Dell patrolled the lower half of the valley, and Foghorn the upper portion. Each rode a thirty-mile circle before midnight, meeting then at the ranch to wolf down a cold meal and change horses. They repeated the circle again, but dawn flushed the sky with clear gold at last, and nothing had happened.

"A lot of sleep lost for nothin'," Foghorn boomed as they rode to the ranch together, hungrily eyeing the smoke from the chuck house chimney.

They were swinging down at the corral when Del's head snapped up, and his red-rimmed eyes hardened as they focused westward. Then he gave a wild whoop that brought Gus and Bill out of the bunkhouse.

"Fire! They sneaked in after we left the range. Great ghosts. It's the winter range! Get blankets from the bunkhouse, get sacks, anything!"

They raided the bunkhouse, and rigged horses with lightning speed. As they swung into the saddle and thundered away, Del gave a groan of dismay. There were three plumes of smoke now, one faint and distant to the north, and another to the south.

A breeze fanned their faces as they topped a swell, and they could see the situation. It was a hopeless one. They were three miles from the fence line of the winter range on the opposite flank of the valley. A roaring column of fire stretched from the fence up into the benches for a mile. It was picking up speed as the breeze caught it. They could hear its dull roar even at that distance. A similar line of red was sweeping down from the head of the valley. A third touch off also had been made southward and was wiping out the brush and grass toward the rim of the bottleneck.

"The winter range is a goner," Del said grimly. "All we can do is to keep it from spreadin' beyond the fence."

Before the smoke shut off vision across the valley, Del saw a group of riders cross a clearing well up on the flank of the Bluestones. They were riding northward to the divide at the head of the valley. Spot Sherill's ranch lay on the prairie beyond the divide.

The four Rolling H men rode for an hour with wet blankets and held back the fire. But the winter range went up in a roaring burst of flame, and the fire rolled on up the Bluestones, to die among the shale slides and rock falls far up the high mountain.

Foghorn, for once, was silent as they met again. He looked furtively at Del, misery in his heart, for he could sense the agony of spirit that was wrenching at the tall young rancher.

"The bones of every critter I own can bleach in this valley, but I'll never sell to Spot Sherill," Del swore grimly.

"We ain't licked yet," Foghorn rumbled hoarsely. "Maybe we

can find a winter range somewhere. Maybe we . . ."

Del gave a bitter laugh. "If there's an acre of grass within a month's drive of the Bluestone country that isn't carryin' its full load of beef right now, I never heard of it. An' we don't dare drive farther than that. Winter would catch us, an' wipe out the herd."

"Say . . . by glory!" Bill Andrews gurgled excitedly. "Yes, there is, Del. Daw-gone, we *have* got a chance. There's some government land on the other side o' the rim, down in Avalanche Valley, that's open. I run into Sam Miller last week in town. He's been runnin' a couple thousand head on a permit over there, but he sold out his brand a month ago, an' went to Texas."

Del whirled. "Sure of it?" he snapped.

Bill nodded, and started to say something, but Del had already reefed his horse and was heading across the valley toward the wagon trail that cut through Lost Creek Hills and joined the main trail to Kearsage beyond. Kearsage, the county seat and the center of the Bluestone country, was twenty-five miles away. "Start roundin' up a bunch for a fast drive!" he called over his shoulder.

Del topped the Lost Creek Hills, and had a bird's-eye view of the rolling range ahead, with the dot along a river in the distance that was the town of Kearsage. The main trail was a yellow ribbon, fading into the horizon. Merging with it three miles out from the hills was the trail from Spot Sherill's Double S Circle. And loping down that trail was a rider on a white horse.

"Sherill," Del murmured as he hurled his own mount down the winding road out of the hills. "I had a hunch he would hear about that grazing lease, too. I got to beat him to town."

Del was riding a wiry, long-legged piebald chestnut, hammer-headed, but close-coupled, with a long, swinging stride and tremendous endurance. Sherill had a lead of a mile when the piebald reached the main trail on the flat. Kearsage was still fifteen miles away, and Sherill had discovered the pursuit, and was pushing his horse.

Sherill's white mount had speed. Del, with grim eyes, saw the distance between them widen. When they had covered half of the route, Sherill was only a speck of dust ahead.

"A mile an' a half an' only seven to go," Del groaned.

But hope began to rise in him again after another grueling mile. His piebald was going like a machine, its long-legged stride never varying. And the white horse was beginning to fail.

The distance between them shrank. Three miles out from town they were separated by less than half a mile. As the lathered, staggering white horse splashed into the river ford, Del was only 100 yards behind. Sherill turned and screeched at Del, but the splashing of the horses drowned him out.

The two animals floundered from the ford and into the dusty street of Kearsage side-by-side, and side-by-side they panted to a halt at the rail in front of the building where the superintendent of rangers was located.

They hurled themselves from their horses, and burst into the ranger's office shoulder to shoulder. The ranger arose from his desk, staring in surprise. Del was grim-eyed, his face lined with fatigue, and blackened by smoke. Sherill was pallid and shaking.

"I got here first, Ranger," Sherill panted hoarsely. "I want to take over that winter grazin' lease in Avalanche Valley."

"I'm applyin' for it, too," Del said sharply.

"First come, first served!" Sherill cried.

"Looks to me like both of you busted in at the same time," the ranger commented.

"But I've got to have it!" Sherill yelled. "I'll pay you double the grass fee. You've got to give it to me. I'm the biggest tax-payer in this county."

"An' the biggest skunk," Del amended. "I'm applyin' for that grass, Ranger, but I can't pay anything more than the regular fee."

The ranger looked from one to the other in perplexity. This was a problem he had never before faced. Sherill continued to plead and threaten. Del remained grimly silent.

"Shut up," the ranger finally snapped to Sherill. "I don't give a whoop if you'll pay ten times the grass fee. That ain't the point. You both got here at the same time. Tell you what I'll do. The first man that gets a herd . . . say, a thousand head . . . on the lease gets the permit. Is that fair?"

"Suits me," Del snapped.

"But not me!" Sherill screeched. "I ain't goin' to race a herd over Avalanche Pass. If a stampede ever started up in that country, every critter would be wiped out."

Avalanche Pass was a saddleback depression on the rim of the Bluestones. It was visible for 100 miles, being 9,000 feet above the plains. It offered the only cattle trail over the mountains, but it was a dangerous one.

"Well, it's up to you," the ranger said. "That's the layout. You've got the edge on Halliday, anyway. Your north range is a couple miles nearer the trail to the pass than Lost Creek Valley. You like a sporting chance, don't you?"

"Nope, he doesn't," Del answered for Sherill. "He only likes a sure thing. I'm startin' back to my spread. I'll drive Avalanche Pass tonight, Sherill, in case you're interested."

"Tonight?" Sherill cried aghast. "You don't dast do it. You'll lose your herd if they start runnin'."

"Wait an' see," Del assured him.

Suddenly Sherill's demeanor changed. "You're on!" he exclaimed. "I'll shove a bunch through the pass tonight, too. I can drive any trail you can, Halliday."

"I'll be on the lease with the permit for the first of you that gets there with a thousand head," the ranger promised.

IV

Del borrowed a fresh horse from a friendly cowpuncher in town and hit the back trail. Sherill was at his heels, also on a borrowed mount. It was mid-afternoon when Del mounted the rim of Lost Creek Hills and overlooked his own spread again. The far side of the valley was only a black scar now. He could see Gus holding a bunch of cattle down near the creek. Foghorn and Bill were working more out of the creek brush. As he rode up, Del estimated the bunch as 600, and they needed 1,000. It would take until dark to reach the required number. He hastily explained the situation as he caught a fresh horse from the remuda, and began helping circle the cattle in.

It was dusk when the 1,000 had been gathered.

"All right," Del said relentlessly. "Start 'em movin'. We ought to make Avalanche Valley by daybreak."

"Sherill's outfit couldn't have done as good, even if they do have more riders," Foghorn boasted. "I betcha we got 'em beat, Del. We'll be in the pass an hour ahead of 'em."

"Maybe," Del admitted. He secretly agreed with Foghorn. But still, the Double S Circle might have worked faster than could be expected. One thing was certain. If they lost this race, Del was ruined.

The herd was hard to start with darkness coming on, but the four riders finally prodded it into motion. They began pushing it as much as they dared without exciting the cattle. Avalanche Pass was dangerous enough for a trail drive under the best of conditions. To take a nervous herd into it at night would be utter suicide.

A five-mile drive along the benches, and over the low, rough ridge at the north end of the valley brought the herd out on the rugged flank of Bluestone Mountain into the moonlight. They were two miles from Avalanche Cañon up which the trail to the high pass mounted.

Foghorn gave a bellow of triumph from the point of the drive. "I told you so, Del. Take a peek back there at the base of the slant south of us."

Del had already seen it—a faint blob of dust rising into the moonlight. A cattle drive.

"Sherill's herd," Foghorn boomed. "We're two miles ahead of 'em. Shucks, we got 'em beat to a whisper."

Del made no comment. Only he of the four saw a rider cross a bench below them and vanish into the shadows of a draw. The rider was traveling fast and heading for Avalanche Cañon.

After an hour, Del's drive reached the cañon, and began ascending it, the rattle of hoofs on rock rising up in a steady, echoing drum. They were in total darkness for half an hour. Then moonlight burnished the tips of 2,000 horns with silver.

At midnight the drive was out of the cañon and puffing up the rugged face of the mountain itself. The range was lost in the moonlight far below, and 2,000 feet higher was Avalanche Pass, but it was still three miles by the zigzag trail. Del looked back and saw the Double S Circle drive emerge on the mountain from the cañon behind them.

After an hour of fast driving, the pass was within reach. The herd was wending around the deep shadow of a small peak when Del came racing up to the point where Foghorn and Gus were riding.

"Swing 'em off the trail," Del said abruptly. "Quick, before they come out into the moonlight again. There's a pocket basin to our left that will hold 'em. Swing 'em, I say . . . don't hold your mouth open, Foghorn!"

"Why . . . what'n hell!" Foghorn gasped weakly. "You'll lose the lead, Del. The Sherill drive ain't far behind us by this time."

Del began swinging the leaders himself. The steers were willing, sensing a chance to rest. Foghorn was numb with dismay, and Bill Andrews and Gus Little came up to protest, but Del glared them down. They dazedly began helping him.

The 1,000 head rattled down a short shale slant, and reached a basin with high walls just big enough to hold them comfortably. The moonlight did not reach them there.

"He's gone loco," Foghorn said despairingly. "This thing has gone to his haid."

But Del seemed sane enough. He grinned thinly as he peered closely at their dumbfounded faces. "You come with me, Foghorn," he instructed. "We'll camp alongside the trail. An' don't talk."

Foghorn brightened. "I knowed it all the time," he snickered. "We're goin' to stampede that other bunch, jest to teach 'em a lesson."

"You're wrong again," Del said.

They returned, dismounted at the bottom of the shale, and went up on foot. They lay in the shelter of a mesquite clump for twenty minutes while the rattle of the approaching herd grew louder.

Then riders and cattle loomed in the darkness. The Double S Circle drive began to flow by with the cowpunchers hazing them along fiercely. Point, swing, and drag, the cattle plodded past like phantoms, except for the *clatter* of the hoofs. They wended into the moonlight beyond and vanished around the peak. Soon they could be heard in the walls of Avalanche Pass above.

"Wal, it's got me hog-tied," Foghorn said in a subdued voice. "We had 'em beat, an' you tossed it away, Del. We might as well turn aroun' an' go home. Why did you do it, boy?"

"Wait," Del cautioned.

Foghorn heard nothing except the occasional *hum* of the

receding herd above, brought by the light night breeze. Then the muffled *rattle* of rifle shots, echoing from the walls of the pass. A heavy jar as though a stick of dynamite had been exploded.

Instantly came a mighty rumble as though thunder was stirring somewhere in these moonlit mountain heads. But it was not thunder. Foghorn had heard that menacing sound too many times to be mistaken.

"Stampede!" he bellowed. "Somebody jumped Sherill's drive. They're runnin'. Daw-gone, what a lucky break! Crimony! Sherill might as well kiss that herd good bye. The other side of the pass is a tangle of ravines that will pile up every critter."

"Let's go back an' start our own bunch through," Del said calmly. "Hustle."

"Sa-ay," Foghorn finally found time to boom as Del's Rolling H steers were once more reluctantly forced into motion, and pouring into the portals of Avalanche Pass. "Who stampeded Sherill's drive? Who done it, hey?"

Del grinned. "I'll give you two guesses," he said.

But Foghorn was relieved from that task. He and Del were riding point, and the drive was well into Avalanche Pass by now. The pass was in darkness, except for stray bands of silvery light here and there where moonlight peered through notches in the walls.

Two riders, coming at a furious lope toward them, had crossed one of those bands of moonlight ahead. Del spurred his horse and advanced to meet them. The riders emerged into a second band of moonlight just as Del reached it. Foghorn breathlessly galloped to the side of his young boss as he recognized the pair ahead.

One was Spot Sherill, wild-eyed and shaking with fury, spouting curses. The other was the squat, sinister form of Frog Durkin. Durkin pushed his horse ahead of Sherill. His voice was thick with rage but deadly as he spoke. "You think you outsmarted me ag'in, eh, Halliday? Well, this is the last trick you'll ever play!"

Durkin's hands swept to his guns. He was a master of the draw. But Del's hand had flashed down and up, smoothly and surely, and so fast that Foghorn saw the red flash of Del's six-shooter before he could even start for his own weapon.

Durkin's right gun slammed wildly, but he was already falling, and his bullet went up into the moonlight. Del's shot had plucked him from the saddle, and he fell to the rocks, rolled over once with a groan, and then lay still.

Spot Sherill had snatched his .45 from its holster and was aiming it at Del when Del's gun slammed once more.

Sherill gave a cry, his gun spurting from his hand. He reeled in the saddle, his arm broken by a bullet.

"I needed you to go with us, so as to make sure that your outfit won't try to stampede *my* herd, too," Del said grimly. "Sherill, you want to make sure that they don't. Savvy."

"I knowed it right from the start," Foghorn boasted to Bill and Gus as the Rolling H drive moved on through Avalanche Pass, with dawn beginning to flush the sky. "Durkin an' his gunslingers had spotted themselves up here to stampede us as we come through. They scouted us while we was down the mountain an' saw that we was in the lead. So, I says to Del . . . 'We'll fool them *hombres*.' So we laid off the trail, an' in the darkness in the pass Durkin stampeded the first herd that showed up. He never guessed we had changed places, until it was too late. Well, it shore was a smart scheme."

"Shore was," Bill agreed. "You tell it so well, I danged near believe you."

★ ★ ★ ★ ★

COLD TRAIL

★ ★ ★ ★

I

Bell Enright fought fierce impatience while he tried to adapt himself to the plodding pace at which cattle travel. The thought came to him that he might be dead within a day or two; in which case what did a few lost minutes matter? There was also the possibility he might be on his way back to prison.

That brought a sinking sensation of horror—the same horror he had known during the seemingly endless eighteen months he had spent in a cell. At least, he reflected, he would have an answer one way or another in a day or two.

It was the last day of March, and a cold rain had slapped bullyingly into his face all day as he and Wilcey Pickens trailed the sixty head of steers and their small saddle string from Bell's range on the Boiling Fork over the divide and down the basin toward the shipping pens at Tamarack. Minaret Peak was lost in the clouds behind them, and here, on the lower toe of the mountain, the fir and pines made a sodden black, dripping mass in the downpour as they drooped over the soiled and withering snowbanks that were the remnants of the departing winter. Bell's worn slicker was letting a trickle of chill rain seep down his spine.

He spoke to Wilcey across the wet backs of the cattle: "With luck we'll have 'em penned and maybe loaded in another two hours. Then we'll learn how deep Paddy O'Toole's hot toddies thaw into a man one at a time."

"Now you've done it," Wilcey complained. "I've been tryin'

to keep my mind off the better things of life . . . like hot tod-dies."

"You'd have thought of it sooner or later," Bell observed.

Wilcey touched his horse and intercepted a flanky, long-legged steer that was making another of its attempts to escape from the column into the timber. "Dang that bunch quitter," Wilcey said mildly. "He won't never give up."

"He only wants to be free," Bell said. And to himself he murmured: "And so do I."

Wilcey was nearing seventy. He was gnarled and gray-thatched and to him weather and the ways of cattle were a part of life to be met with tolerance. He understood these things, but Bell knew he did not understand why they were driving sixty head of steers to the shipping pens on the last day of March. This was no season of the year to sell northern beef. The steers were in fair condition, considering the hard winter, but at best they would not bring much above bottom price.

But Wilcey asked no questions. He lived alone, hunting, fish-ing, and trapping wolves for bounty and hiring out at roundups when the mood suited him. His help in driving Bell's cattle to Tamarack was voluntary. Only a few people in the Minaret country would go out of their way to assist Josh Enright's son. Owen Randolph was one. He was so big a man he could choose his friends without fear of censure. Alice Drake was another. Bell now let his mind linger on the luxury of that thought.

They emerged from the thinning timber and the vast sweep of the basin lay before them. Tamarack stood nakedly on the flat down the sloping bench. In the railroad yard a switch engine sent smoke rings spinning above the roofs where the wind dis-solved them.

The railroad right of way came to meet them, climbing the slight grade to their level in a graceful loop. It crossed their path scarcely 200 yards ahead, then headed south toward the South

Fork bridge. North of town there were no rails—nothing but a line of stakes that dwindled into the distance. Those stakes were old and weather-beaten, for the Mid-Continent & Western had been forced to pause for nearly two years in Minaret Basin to refinance before proceeding with its plan to tap the rich cattle and wheat country on the high plains to the west.

Wilcey pointed. "Ain't that a new canvas top there north o' the depot? Dance hall most likely. Looks like it's true that Mid C aims to start layin' track ag'in this summer."

The cattle were showing uneasiness. Bell rode ahead to steady the leaders. "It's the railroad tracks that's making 'em spooky," he said. "They've never seen such a thing. I'd hate to have 'em start running here. Too much brush and many cutbanks. It'll be safer if we swing north and shove through town to the pens."

Wilcey looked dubious. "Folks won't like it." He shrugged.

"Other men drive cattle down Main Street," Bell said.

"These other fellers ain't named Enright," Wilcey replied. "An' Pete Jennings won't like it, either. There's an ordinance ag'in' it. Jennings is likely to enforce it when he sees it's you."

Bell looked at the distant town. He was twenty-six, a man with thick, dark hair and dark eyes, flat-shouldered and sinewy of waist and long and lean of leg. Beneath his slicker he wore a short duck saddle jacket that had seen much service and woolen saddle pants, cuffed over his spurred boots. He had a solid jaw and chin and carried the remoteness of a person accustomed to making his way alone. There was a deep flame of challenge in his dark gaze. This was the only outward relic prison had left on him. The revulsion he felt when he thought of those days behind bars he kept carefully hidden. All he wanted to show the world was his defiance and none of the hurt.

"You'll get no place buckin' everybody," Wilcey warned.

Bell hesitated. He couldn't afford to pay a fine now. Not even the $25 and costs that might be assessed.

"All right," he said with an effort. "We'll put 'em across the tracks right here and go in the back way. This is as good a place as any."

They crowded the steers into a compact column and began hazing them. They might have made it by sheer momentum, but, as they got the cattle in motion, a locomotive whistle sounded in the distance. A train, bound for Tamarack, was approaching, unseen because the tracks entered a cut nearby.

"Swing 'em away!" Bell snapped. "I'll try to flag that blasted engine down before it stampedes 'em."

He spurred his horse onto the tracks. Now he could see the train approaching. He waved his hat, then pulled off his slicker, and whirled that, too. He heard the clash of metal as the engineer applied his brakes. The whistle sounded. It was an accommodation train composed of a mail and baggage car, a passenger coach, and a string of boxcars.

The train slowed. Bell raced to join Wilcey in chasing the cattle away from the tracks. The steers were bellowing and trying to make up their minds whether to run. But they still were under control.

The engine and the passenger coach emerged from the cut and ground to a stop. Passengers gazed from the windows. Bell saw a young woman in the coach. She was looking at him impersonally with eyes that were gray and clear and very cool. Her hair was a deep auburn and worn long in the fashion of the day. High cheek bones above slim cheeks gave her face a distinctive beauty. She had a small nose whose set was somewhat on the aggressive side and a good mouth with a moist underlip. She was stylishly dressed and seemed to be alone, for she had draped her sealskin jacket over the back of the worn plush seat at her side.

Wilcey had seen, too. "Nancy Carmody," he murmured as he and Bell continued pushing the nervous cattle farther from this steaming monster that had appeared before them. "She's home at last for the readin' of her grandpaw's will, I reckon. You remember her, Bell. She's a wild one." Wilcey added in a soft and longing tone: "She's somethin', ain't she? A gray-eyed redhead with a figure. I've heard say she can bend men aroun' her fingers without half tryin'. I can believe it."

"At your age you better not set your sights any higher than hot toddies," Bell said.

An angry voice was shouting at them. The engineer was brandishing a fist. His name was Sim Gillis, and he was a large, leathery, loud-mouthed individual.

"Do you mean to say you had the gall to flag me down jest because of a bunch of cows?" Gillis was roaring. "You're that Enright fella, ain't you? Don't get any notions that you've got folks buffaloed in this country."

Gillis leaped to the throttle and gave the engine steam. The drive wheels spun. He yanked a cord and the whistle erupted into a deafening uproar.

That did it. The steers broke like frightened children, heading for the timber. Bell and Wilcey hurled their horses into breakneck pursuit. Bell's animal crashed through scrub cedar, vaulted a boulder, and lurched into a shallow wash that was one of the many that veined this eroded area. Tree branches raked his hat from his head, and the snag end of a dead branch ripped his slicker.

He looked back. The train was rolling again. Sim Gillis was guffawing and enjoying the spectacle.

A steer hit a deadfall and went end over end, breaking its neck. Another crashed into a boulder and Bell saw it hobbling on a broken leg when he looked back.

After a mile he and Wilcey caught up with the leaders and forced them into a milling circle. When the bulk of the steers had halted, they moved out to round up a half dozen critters that had scattered into the brush.

Bell shot the steer with the broken leg and did the same for another that had fallen into a coulée. The stampede had cost him three head of stock. The others were brush-scarred and all had lost weight.

"We'll never get them to cross the tracks now," he said. "We'll have to drive right down Main Street to the pens whether people like it or not."

It was late afternoon when they reached the first outscattering of buildings on the fringe of town. Tamarack had been in existence since the first herds came up from Texas to stock northern range, but it had never been more than a crossroads cow town of a half dozen buildings until two years in the past. At that time the railroad had driven a spur into the basin from Marleyville, which was the county seat on the transcontinental line ninety miles south. Mid C had intended to build on northward out of the basin through Round Valley, and then veer west to the open plains along the Brulé River.

Tamarack's population had grown to 1,000 in a week's time, and eventually passed the 3,000 mark. Then the railroad had struck a snag. The construction crews had pulled out overnight, and the knockdown gambling houses and dance halls that had lined Front Street vanished with them. Now two thirds of the buildings in Tamarack were empty.

The steers had forgotten most of their fright, but the sight of the houses now began to worry them. Bell and Wilcey quickened the pace and brought the animals into the head of Main Street at a lumbering trot. The red-painted depot stood at the opposite end of the business section, and south of it near Front Street were the corrals and loading chutes.

The rain had ceased and some of the citizens of the town had emerged. Two housewives, shawls over their heads and market baskets on their arms, were picking their way across the muddy thoroughfare. At sight of the oncoming cattle they gathered their skirts and fled in a panic.

Other women came to their doors and screamed warnings to their children. Men appeared and glared angrily at the lumbering herd when they recognized Bell. Owen Randolph appeared in the doorway of his office and shook his head reprovingly. Owen, a lawyer and prosperous land dealer, was one of Tamarack's most respected citizens. Always in spotless linen and a gray business suit, he had a fine, young-old face beneath hair and brows that were cotton white.

"It couldn't be helped, Owen," Bell said as he rode past.

Steers trotted through the dust of the street and overflowed onto the sidewalks until everyone on Main Street was driven to cover.

Pete Jennings came hurrying from his deputy sheriff's office, frowning forbiddingly. "You know better'n this, Enright!" he yelled. "I'll book you for this."

Sim Gillis, the engineer who had stampeded the cattle on the bench, emerged from a saloon a dozen yards away. Gillis was carrying his heavy metal lunch pail.

Bell left the saddle instantly. "And you'll know better the next time, too, Gillis," he said.

Gillis saw what was coming and set himself, kicking and throwing a punch at Bell in the same motion. Bell took the toe of the heavy shoe on his thigh, batted the fist aside, and swung, first with his left, and then with his right, hitting his target both times. Gillis staggered, but got his balance and swung savagely with the lunch pail. Bell ducked but the pail glanced from his shoulder with numbing force.

Then he smashed a left deeply into Gillis's ribs and brought up his right to Gillis's jaw. The railroad man reeled back and sat down, his mouth sagging open. All the fight suddenly drained out of him.

It had all happened so quickly that Pete Jennings had not arrived in time to interfere. Bell swung back into the saddle and stared harshly at the deputy. "If there's a fine for that, too, I'll take care of it after I load these cattle," he said.

"There'll be a fine," Jennings assured him angrily. "Now it's assault an' battery on top of the other one."

At that precise moment Bell noticed Alice Drake. She worked in Owen Randolph's office as clerk and secretary. She had come to the window, a pencil thrust in her hair, and a pen in her hand. She wore a neat white blouse with sleeve protectors and a very practical dark skirt. A gold watch was pinned to her bosom. She had very nice blue eyes, golden yellow hair, and a clear-skinned oval face with a small firm chin.

Her lips were framing a dismayed exclamation. Bell knew what she was saying, for he had heard it before. "Oh, Bell, why did you do that?"

A steer went lurching across the sidewalk, and then up the wooden steps that led to the door of the Mountain House, Tamarack's best hotel. The steer might have leaped through the only plate glass window in town and into the midst of startled diners in the eating room, but a young woman suddenly appeared from the door of the establishment and confronted the animal.

It was Nancy Carmody, the gray-eyed, auburn-haired girl who had been aboard the train. At her heels loomed a stalwart, handsome blond man who wore expensive range garb and a flat-crowned, wide-brimmed hat. He sported a small, clipped yellow mustache. His name was Leach Valentine. He was in his middle thirties and had been in the Minaret country only half a dozen years. Flashy of manner, with a white-toothed smile and gifted with persuasive vocal powers, Leach Valentine had worked for a time as a rider at Spearhead. He and Buck Carmody had not seen eye to eye on some matters, and Valentine had moved on. Later, he had served as Owen Randolph's aid in operating small cow outfits that Owen had taken over in the course of his operations as land speculator.

After Buck Carmody's death, Owen, who was acting as temporary administrator of the estate pending the reading of the cattleman's will, had appointed Valentine foreman of the big Spearhead outfit, to the astonishment of the other ranchers in the county. Valentine had been one of Nancy Carmody's most ardent suitors before her parting with her grandfather. Apparently he was now losing no time in resuming his attentions.

She could have stepped back, leaving the matter of the blundering steer in his hands for he had already drawn his six-shooter and was trying to slide past her to get a shot at the animal, but she pushed the weapon aside.

"There's no need of that, Leach!" she said sharply. She shrugged off his restraining grasp and faced the steer herself. She was carrying her handsome sealskin jacket on her arm. As the steer loomed close to her, she shook out the garment and draped it over the horns. The steer, blinded, reared in fright. Then it came down on its four hoofs again, trying to shake off the terrifying object.

Nancy Carmody snatched the jacket away. Then she gathered her skirts high and kicked the steer impudently on the snout with the toe of her high-heeled slipper. The animal immediately wheeled and went plunging down the steps and rejoined its companions.

II

Nancy Carmody laughed gleefully, but Valentine was scowling. "Damn it, Nan," he complained, "you made a spectacle of yourself. Furthermore, you might have got hurt."

She looked at Deputy Pete Jennings who was helping Sim Gillis to his feet across the street. "He had it coming, Deputy!" she called. "In fact, he got off easy. My granddad would have put a bullet in him for what he did." She eyed Bell with cool dispassion. "And so would Josh Enright, from what I've been told," she added.

She walked away then. Valentine took her arm. "How soon am I to be led to the slaughter?" she asked.

Bell rode out of hearing. Wilcey looked back and murmured yearningly: "She's grown into such a looker it's almost wicked. She's got the devil in her. Her maw was a dance-hall singer, an' thet's where the wildness comes from, I suppose."

Bell saw Valentine escort the auburn-haired girl into the door of Owen Randolph's office. All eyes along the street followed her. Womenfolk peered from the corners of doors and around lifted curtains. Some were exchanging scathing glances and whispering behind their hands. The expressions on masculine faces were quite different. Bell remembered what Wilcey had said about Nancy Carmody's being able to twist men around her slim fingers.

"Looks like they're fixin' to read Buck Carmody's will," Wilcey said. "All the old-timers from Spearhead who expect to be remembered are gatherin'. Maybe they figure they'll inherit the whole shebang. I wonder why Nancy Carmody bothered to come back home for the readin'. Everybody says she's sure to be cut off with only a dollar."

Bell was recalling Nancy Carmody's remark about his own father. He was surprised that she had spoken to him at all. That had never happened before, even though they had been born and raised only twenty miles apart. She had been the grand-daughter of Buck Carmody, the strong-willed man who had built the Spearhead brand to a high place in the sun. Bell's father on the other hand had been Josh Enright, formerly leader of the outlaw band known as the Enright Wild Bunch. Spearhead ran 10,000 head of cattle in the basin to the south and on the rich range along Clear Fork River as far west as the Divide. The Enright holdings consisted of a small brand and a series of range and homestead rights along the wild valley of the Boiling Fork River that drained into the basin to the north.

Nancy Carmody's mother had died the day she was born. There was scandal connected with that occasion for it was said it had taken place in a house of questionable reputation in Marleyville. Her father, who had been Buck Carmody's only son, had died only a year later. Frank Carmody had drunk himself to death.

Nancy Carmody had never attended the little Tamarack school where Bell had been an unwanted pupil. She had been educated by private tutors at Spearhead and at finishing schools in the East and abroad. When she was eighteen, she was acting as mistress of Spearhead. Buck Carmody was an important man in the state and Cottonwood House, his rambling mansion that overlooked his corrals and branding chutes at his headquarters ranch on the Clear Fork was often the scene of pretentious social affairs in honor of visiting notables. Even a President of the United States had once been Buck Carmody's guest for elk hunting while Nancy acted as hostess.

Bell had passed her often on the trails—a wild-riding, proud, and lonely girl, who galloped at breakneck speed on one of her grandfather's thoroughbreds, her auburn hair streaming behind her like a flame in the sun. She had always seemed driven by some need that would never let her remain content. And never had she given the slightest indication that she was aware such common clay as Bell Enright existed.

Suddenly, at the age of twenty, she had thrown off Buck Carmody's iron hand and had left Spearhead and the Minaret.

That had been four years ago. After a time Tamarack was shocked to hear that she had become an actress and was singing and dancing in a bold musical play. She was reported in Chicago, and then in New York, and finally in Paris. Within the past few months a new flood of rumors had swept Tamarack. It was whispered that the real reason she and her grandfather had parted was because she had engaged in a clandestine affair with a visitor at Cottonwood House. It was said she was leading a fast and lurid life abroad. Her name was being mentioned in connection with men who were notorious for their amorous adventures.

Buck Carmody had died about the time these things began to be talked about. That had been nearly two months ago. He had been given the biggest funeral in the history of the range. It had taken time for the news to reach Nancy Carmody in Europe, and for her to return by ship and rail. Now she was home after four years.

"Did you see her ankles?" Wilcey was murmuring with awe. "Neat, wasn't they?"

"The world's full of ankles," Bell said. "Two to a person. I wish I had those three steers alive."

They crowded the cattle into the railroad pens. Cars were waiting at the loading chutes.

"Better load your critters right away," the yardmaster informed Bell. "We'll hook you onto the southbound freight, which won't be leavin' till eight o'clock, but I want to clear this sidin' as soon as possible."

It took an hour of prodding to get the tired steers into the cars. When Bell closed the door of the last car, he said: "I've got business to take care of, Wilcey. I'll tell Paddy to line up toddies for you. I'll be along later."

He turned to walk away, but a very tall and lean man blocked his path. He pulled up. "Hello, Irons," he said slowly. "So you're back in Tamarack?"

"Since yesterday." The man nodded. He added, without change of tone: "We don't like to have Mid C men roughed up, Enright. We sure don't." His voice was soft and carried a velvet Kentucky drawl.

"No?" Bell said evenly, his eyes bright and hard.

The other man sighed. He had seemed taller than Bell, but he found himself only at eye level. "I don't say that maybe it wasn't comin' to Sim Gillis," he said. "I only want to know why."

"Ask Gillis," Bell said.

"I'll ask him," the man nodded. "I really will."

They stood measuring each other. The man confronting Bell was Clay Irons, who held the title of assistant construction superintendent of Mid-Continent. The title was misleading. Clay Irons's job was to maintain order in the turbulent railroad camps—with fists or guns as the occasion demanded.

Men who feared Irons referred to him behind his back as a paid killer. It was said the brace of six-shooters, whose bulges were visible beneath the skirts of his dark, sack coat, had sent six men to their graves. Irons had the eyes of his calling, pale gray and webbed at the corners by small crow's-foot puckers. He wore a dark funnel-brimmed range hat, a soft flannel shirt, and black tie. His hair was sandy in color and his skin had been browned by long exposure to sun and wind. He was thirty but looked much older. He had served a hitch in the cavalry after he had run away from home in the Blue Grass at the age of sixteen. Afterward he had been hunter, cowboy, and prospector, and marshal of wild boomtowns. Now he was the strong right arm of Mid C in its construction activities.

Men said Irons was living on borrowed time, for he had made many enemies. Trouble was his profession. He was no stranger in Tamarack, having wielded discipline over the construction camps when Mid C was building into the basin. He had pulled out for other ends of steel when the railroad had halted work at Tamarack. Now he was back.

"I'll be in town and easy to find for the next three, four hours in case you hanker to look me up again," Bell said.

He moved forward. Irons's eyes chilled. Then he moved aside and out of the way.

"Man alive, but you pick 'em tough," Wilcey growled as he fell in step with Bell. "What if Irons had decided not to give trail when you walked at him?"

"I wouldn't know," Bell said.

"Wal I do!" Wilcey snorted. "Both o' you'd have got hurt. You're both tough an' proud. Well, Irons showin' up here proves one thing for certain. Mid C has raised fresh money an' aims to start buildin' ag'in. Ain't no doubt about it now. That means Spearhead will be worth two, three times what it was. Too bad Buck Carmody didn't live to see it."

A rumor had swept the range a few weeks earlier that the right of way Mid C had staked northward beyond town was a fake. This was now accepted as a fact. Everyone now knew that the railroad survey ended at the Boiling Fork, north of town. Beyond that point lay wild, gorge-cut Round Valley, and to the west of Round Valley loomed the Red Mountains, which were in reality a maze of eroded buttes, difficult of access. It was said Mid C had finally realized that costs would be too high to build through Round Valley. Everyone was now in on the secret. And the secret was that the only feasible route was by way of the Cedar Fork River, across Spearhead range and through the Reds south and west of Minaret Peak.

Official announcement would come only from Henry Driscoll, president of the railroad whose offices were in Omaha. However, it was whispered that Driscoll had secretly visited Buck Carmody the previous fall before the rancher's fatal illness. It was then that the deal for a right of way across Spearhead range was said to have been made. If the railroad built by way of the Clear Fork, the route would be diverted westward a dozen miles south of Tamarack. A new town would rise and Spearhead would own the site. All its other holdings along the route would soar in value. Tamarack would be doomed to become a ghost town. In fact, it was already on its way to that status. The rush to get out from under had already started.

III

Bell left Wilcey and walked to Owen Randolph's office. Pete Jennings stood, waiting on the sidewalk, and said: "Thanks to Owen's request I'll overlook it this time, Enright. Owen said he'd talk to you about this habit you Enrights have of tryin' to hurrah this town."

Jennings, like Clay Irons, wore two pistols. Bell looked at Jennings, and then at his two guns, and walked on. He wore no weapon in town. It was part of the pledge he had made when pardoned from prison.

He entered Owen Randolph's tile-floored main office. Alice sat at a desk behind the business counter. She arose quickly and came to face him across this barrier. Her eyes were very blue and very clear. And very expressive. They mirrored her thoughts, but she was unaware of this, fondly believing she was a very obtuse young woman. Bell braced himself to meet the reproof she had in mind for him.

She was very careful to keep this out of her voice. "Hello, Bell," she said.

She stood waiting for an explanation and a defense, if he had any to offer. She was a small, dainty woman. He could see across the top of her carefully brushed golden hair. It was drawn tightly back and held by a shell comb at the back. He suddenly began

41

visualizing the beauty of that gorgeous hair loose, falling about her shoulders and blowing like a golden cloud in the wind and sunshine.

Her gaze rose to his and she sensed the trend of his thoughts. Color swarmed furiously up from her slim throat.

"You are trying to think of ways to lecture me without letting me know I'm being dressed down, Alice," he said.

She bridled a trifle. She had a temper, but imagined that she held it always in a tight, lady-like rein. "Was it necessary to antagonize the town by bringing your cattle down Main Street?" she demanded. "In addition, you had to start a brawl right in front of everyone."

"What you mean is that I acted just like an Enright," he said grimly.

This was not the first time they had clashed. Conflicting thoughts played across her piquant features like the fleeting passage of cloud shadows across a fair land. She had always been unswerving in her views of what was right and wrong, and she particularly abhorred violence. Yet, he sensed an uncertainty in her, a doubt in her own precepts. Her mother had told him that Alice had prayed for him each night he had been in prison. She had written many times to the governor to intercede in the case. Bell believed it was these appeals to the governor as well as her influence on Owen Randolph that had eventually won him a pardon. For that he would forever be in her debt.

Willis Drake, her father, operated a prosperous freighting business in Tamarack. In fact, Alice had been born in Minaret Basin. She had attended the one-room school, and, although Bell had been older and two grades above her, she had gone out of her way to be kind to the dark-eyed, defiant boy who had been avoided by other children because he was the son of the outlaw, Josh Enright.

Two years ago Bell had asked her to marry him. Alice had

delayed her answer, and, during that interval, Bell had been arrested, convicted, and sent to prison. Now he knew there was still a dark doubt in her mind. She was aware he was still awaiting an answer. And he knew, also, that she had decided that the answer was up to him. If she was to marry him, he must put all his wildness behind him.

"Why are you marketing cattle now, Bell?" she asked.

"I need a little ready cash," he said. "Where's Owen?"

"Still in the inner office. They're reading Buck Carmody's will. They should be finished soon. What do you mean, you need cash? Winter's over. Surely you can get along until your cattle fatten and bring a better price?"

"It's a business deal that won't wait," he said.

"Not land speculation?" she cried protestingly. "Don't do that, Bell. You have no idea how much people in this town have lost in land gambling."

She waited for him to explain. When he did not, her features took on a hurt expression. He reached out, took her hand in an instinctive gesture of contrition. It was a firm hand, warm and small, but unyielding.

"You can't always add up everyone like a column of figures, Alice," he told her.

"How else can you know a person except by adding up the list of his actions, good or bad?" she demanded.

The door of the inner office opened. Nancy Carmody came into the main room, followed by Owen Randolph and Leach Valentine and half a dozen other persons. Among the group Bell saw Jenny Walking Elk, the plump Brulé woman who had been nurse and maid to Nancy Carmody from childhood.

A small, taut smile rode Nancy Carmody's lips as though she had found something bitterly humorous in what had taken place. Valentine took her arm and said: "Your grandfather meant it for the best, darling."

"That depends on how you look at it." She shrugged. "Grandfather always wanted to run my life like he ran Spearhead . . . efficiently and strictly according to his views on improvement of the blood lines of the ranch stock."

"We'll talk it over tomorrow," Valentine said. "After all, you should be pleased with the will. You're too tired to go out to Spearhead tonight. I've hired the bridal suite at Mountain House for you. Jenny will be with you, of course."

The group walked to the street then.

Alice looked excitedly at Bell. "That sounds like Nan Carmody might have inherited Spearhead, after all," she breathed, her eyes dancing. "If so, I'm glad."

"Glad? Why?"

"All the busybodies in town have been predicting she'd be cut off entirely. You know what they've been saying about her. A woman can't defend herself against such talk."

"Are you siding in with her against the busybodies?" Bell grinned, surprised.

Alice shrugged. "I don't imagine Nan Carmody needs help from me," she said, and it seemed to him there was a deep current of wistful resentment in her voice. "She is able to take care of herself. She . . . she has everything. Even Spearhead evidently."

Owen Randolph returned from speeding his departing clients. He was in high good humor, his sun-browned face jovial beneath his distinctive mane of prematurely white hair. He was a tall, straight-shouldered, vigorous man. In his middle fifties he was as light of stride as a person half his age.

He had come to Tamarack nearly ten years ago. It was common belief that he was from an aristocratic Eastern family and had come West for his health. He had pale hazel brown eyes set deeply beneath his white brows. His features were clean-shaven, and cast in a bold, almost harsh mold. But it was his eyes one remembered. They were as inscrutable in the courtroom or in a business deal as they were at a poker table. Indeed, Owen had more than held his own at the gambling tables in Tamarack in his early days. But he had long since given up such pastimes. He was now a well-to-do businessman. He still practiced law, and had represented many of the leading cattle outfits in the county, including Buck Carmody's Spearhead, but his land dealings now occupied the bulk of his time.

His face became serious when he looked at Bell, and he wagged an admonitory finger at him. "Why do you insist on rubbing people's fur the wrong way, son?" he asked plaintively. "Alice, can't you tame him down? I had to talk fast and meek to Pete Jennings to keep him out of jail."

"I'd like a word with you, Owen," Bell said.

Owen eyed him questioningly, then led the way into the rear office. Bell closed the door. "I need twenty-five hundred dollars," he said. "At once."

Owen's brows arched. He motioned Bell into a smaller inner office. "No one can eavesdrop on us in this one," he murmured as he bolted the door.

He seated himself at a desk and offered a cigar humidor. Bell shook his head, preferring to roll a cigarette. Owen himself never smoked.

"Did you mean that you need that much money on top of what those cattle will bring?" Owen asked.

"Only part of it, if I can market the beef in a hurry," Bell said. "I'm hoping I can sell them to a commission house at Marleyville. If not, I'll need the entire amount."

Owen was frowning dubiously.

"I'll sign a lien against the rest of the stock at E Loop," Bell said. "There are approximately one hundred and eighty head of cattle, nineteen horses. You already hold the mortgage Dad signed against the land."

"Are you in trouble with the law again?" Owen asked.

"Not yet, at least," Bell said.

"Do you want to tell me about it? Does it have anything to do with your father?"

Bell hesitated. He trusted Owen. Except for Alice he felt that the lawyer was the only person who had ever lifted a finger to help him. Owen had told him it was his influence that had prevailed on the governor to issue a pardon after Bell had served a year and a half of a five-year prison term.

Owen had also been a friend of Bell's father. It was Owen who had penned the letters that Josh Enright had dictated to be sent to his son in prison. Owen had read Bell's letters to his father. For Josh Enright had never learned to read or write. And Owen already carried a mortgage of $7,000 on E Loop's range rights. Josh Enright had acquired title to a modest stretch of graze on the Boiling Fork in country so rough other cattlemen avoided it. Bell had not known about the encumbrance until his father's death the previous fall when he was still in prison. Josh Enright evidently had needed the money for some purpose he had not cared to reveal even to his own son. He had borrowed it from Owen three years in the past, and, although the principal was now due in less than thirty days, Bell's mind was at rest on that score, for Owen had assured him he would renew.

He only shrank from placing Owen in a position that was contrary to his principles. But he needed advice. "Yes," he said. "It's about Josh. It started about two weeks ago when I received this by mail."

He drew from his coat a message. It was written with a pencil on cheap, ruled paper.

Owen read it aloud. " 'If you are interested in learning who killed Josh Enright and why, then get in touch personally with Matt Barker, who is a prisoner in the county jail at Marleyville. Tell nobody else about this.' " Owen's eyes lifted, frowning. "No signature," he commented. "And so . . . ?"

"I went to Marleyville," Bell said. "Matt Barker is in jail there, sure enough. He's held for killing a tinhorn gambler in a honky-tonk row. I talked to him privately. Barker claims he once rode with my father in Josh's outlaw days."

"Not that again," Owen protested. "You were convicted once of helping one of your father's lawless friends."

"Barker lied, of course," Bell said. "He's just another old scoundrel trying to build up a rep by posing as having been an Enright longrider. Robbing drunken men is his real long suit. This time, however, he actually killed a man. He says it was self-defense. I looked up the story in the Marleyville newspaper and he may be telling the truth. But the only witnesses were buddies of the tinhorn, and Barker is sure they'll swear him to the gallows. His trial comes up Saturday at Marleyville. That's the day after tomorrow."

"But what about your father's death?" Owen asked.

"Barker said he'd tell me who killed Josh and the reason why it was done if I helped him escape the jail. The way will be greased if I turn over twenty-five hundred dollars to a certain person who is on duty at the jail. That must be done at once, for this person goes off the night shift after Saturday, and won't be on it again for thirty days. By that time Barker figures he'll be in the death cell at the state pen."

"Surely you aren't going to be taken in by a yarn like that?" Owen snorted.

"Barker says he was hanging around Tamarack last fall," Bell went on. "He claims he was riding up the bench trail and had pulled off into the brush at Moccasin Creek ford to cook a bait of grub. My guess is that he was hunkered there in the hope of holding up some teamster or rider. He said two men came riding through the brush and waited at the ford until Josh Enright came along. They seemed to be talking in a friendly manner.

Without warning one of them pulled out a pistol and shot my father point-blank. Afterward, it began to snow and all tracks were wiped out, including Barker's."

"Incredible!" Owen declared. "It's only a scheme to bamboozle you into getting him out of jail."

"I'm sure he knows something," Bell insisted. "He showed me a ring. It bears a carved lion's head with a small blue stone in its mouth. Josh always wore it. My mother had given it to him."

Owen shrugged. "Barker probably came upon your father's body later on, and robbed it," he said. "Surely you aren't really going through with this hare-brained scheme, Bell? Think what it would mean if you're caught. You were convicted once of giving shelter and help to a desperado. I wangled a pardon for you once, but you know what would happen if you were mixed up in another such affair. They'd give you the limit."

"I know the risks," Bell said.

He now regretted that he had told Owen the story. He had hoped the lawyer would understand. Everyone had taken the same indifferent attitude when Josh Enright had been slain. They had accepted the common explanation—some grudge from the old outlaw days had caught up with him at last.

"Josh Enright likely made more enemies in the past than you could count on the toes of a centipede," Pete Jennings had said. "Time don't wipe out some grudges, an' outlaw blood don't ever turn into kitten milk, either. I proved that two years ago when I caught Josh's son hangin' out with one of his dad's old longriders."

Pete Jennings had been disappointed when he had failed to send Josh Enright back to prison along with Bell on a charge of harboring a fugitive from the law. It so happened that Bell's father had an iron-clad alibi the night Bell had been arrested. Josh Enright had been a patient at Buck Carmody's Spearhead ranch house, nursing a broken leg he had sustained that same afternoon when his horse had fallen while he was working at calf roundup with a Spearhead wagon.

Bell stood thinking of these things as he watched the frowning disapproval in Owen's face.

"Twenty-five hundred dollars is a lot of money," Owen said dryly.

"Worth it to me," Bell said. "Josh didn't deserve to die like that. The man who killed him doesn't deserve to live."

"What about Alice?" Owen asked.

Bell straightened a little.

"She's overlooked the prison incident, believing you were unjustly sentenced. But she wouldn't overlook a second mistake on your part."

"You mean you know there's still a doubt in her mind, but that I might have been mixed up in that bank robbery with Tom Buell, after all," Bell said grimly. He looked closer at Owen. "And in your mind, also, Owen," he added.

Owen slapped a palm angrily on the desk. "Damn it, Bell, now you are trying to antagonize me."

"Get me the money, Owen," Bell said. "In greenbacks, not gold. And make out the lien on my stock."

Owen spread his hands helplessly. "It will take a little time. I'll have to go to the bank."

Bell waited half an hour. Then Owen returned by way of the rear door and handed him several packets of bills. He signed the paper Owen placed before him and stored the money in the pockets of his saddle coat. "Thanks, Owen," he said, then opened the door and walked into the main office.

Clay Irons was standing at the counter, talking to Alice. Irons had his black, steeple-crowned hat tilted back on his head, and he was relaxed and smiling. He was saying in his soft voice: "Yeah, it's been two long years. I figured you'd be married, Alice. It's right pleasant to find that things don't change too much, except that you've grown even prettier than ever."

Alice laughed gaily at him, her elbows on the counter, her chin cupped in her hands. Glowing like a light within her was the pleased and half-frightened awareness of a woman who found herself the subject of a man's intense purpose.

Then Alice became aware of Bell's presence. She straightened. Irons turned, also, and stood leaning against the counter.

"I'll be back from Marleyville in two days, with luck," Bell said.

"I'll count on you for Saturday night," Alice said. "There's to be a sociable and a dance at Woodman's Hall to raise funds for the Ladies Aid. I'm on the committee."

Bell felt a thrust of emotion. Alice's frank eyes did not waver. He understood this was her way of telling him that his probation was over and that she was at last inviting him into her world where she could stand with him and face the past and the opinions of others. There was a hopeful question in her eyes—and a darkening shadow of trouble, too. He guessed she sensed there were reservations in his mind, and that he stood at some crossroad in life.

"Only calamity will keep me away," he said. "I'll call for you Saturday evening at seven."

IV

He moved to the street. Irons tipped his hat to Alice and joined him on the sidewalk. The clouds were lifting. The damp breeze brought the heady fragrance of a mountain land that was awakening from winter.

"I hear your father is dead," Irons said. "Murdered."

"Yes," Bell replied tersely.

"I'm sorry," Irons said. "I talked to Josh Enright a time or two. And to old-time peace officers who knew him. They all respected him. And so did I. There wasn't a drop of killer blood in him."

He went silent a moment then. Bell guessed that he hadn't meant to use that word—killer. It evidently produced a bitterness in his thoughts.

"Pete Jennings tells me nobody has any idea who did it," Irons said.

"None," Bell answered. "At least up to now."

"Then you're still lookin', I take it?"

"I'll never quit looking," Bell said.

"I talked to Miss Nancy Carmody since I last spoke to you," Irons went on. "She told me what happened up on the bench. Cattle are a big item in Mid C's income. We don't like to antagonize our customers. I'll talk to Sim Gillis. You'll be paid for the steers you lost if you'll file a claim." Irons added: "You're a mighty lucky man. If I was in your boots, nothin' in heaven an' earth could stop me from escortin' Miss Alice to that dance Saturday. She'd be mighty disappointed if you didn't show up."

Irons strolled away then. Bell stood, gazing thoughtfully after the Kentuckian's tall thin figure. Then he headed for Paddy O'Toole's place to join Wilcey.

A moment later Owen Randolph stepped from his office wearing his bowler hat and carrying his walking stick. He made sure Bell had passed out of sight, then walked briskly across the street and entered the barroom of the Mountain House.

Leach Valentine sat at a card table reading an old copy of a Denver newspaper. Also at the table and scowling heavily over a game of solitaire was a heavy-jowled, thick-lipped rider named Shep Murdock. A bottle and glasses stood before them.

Shep Murdock had been hired as a rider at Spearhead not long after Owen had appointed Valentine as acting foreman. He had thick, heavy, swart features. Dark, greasy hair curled from beneath the grime of his hat. He carried a six-shooter. Since Valentine had been named foreman at Spearhead, the pair of them had become inseparable. Both were friends of Deputy Sheriff Pete Jennings. In fact, they spent much of their time when in town in the deputy's office playing stud poker for small stakes with Jennings.

Owen ordered rye and water at the bar. Valentine arose and joined him. They talked casually of the weather for a moment until the bartender had moved out of hearing.

"Come to the inner office in five minutes," Owen murmured. "Bring Murdock along. Come by the back way. Don't be seen."

"But I'm waiting on Nancy," Valentine objected.

"This is important," Owen breathed. "Very important."

"But, if I'm going to marry . . . ," Valentine began angrily.

Owen downed his drink, tossed a coin on the bar, and walked out. Presently Valentine and Shep Murdock left the Mountain House, also.

In Paddy O'Toole's saloon two blocks east, Bell was taking his first sip of a steaming toddy.

"Did you hear the news?" Wilcey asked. "Buck Carmody left Spearhead to the red-headed girl after all. Everything from hoofs to horns. But with a big string on it."

"String?"

"Nancy Carmody has to be married within thirty days or the whole danged caboodle goes to charity," Wilcey said. "An' married to a resident o' Minaret Basin at that. Ain't that something? It was like old Buck to have the last word. He made sure Spearhead won't fall into the paws of one of them dudes she was runnin' herd with back East an' acrost the pond. If she wants the ranch, she's got to stay tied down to this country."

"'Tis Leach Valentine who will be the lucky man," Paddy O'Toole said. "Sure, an' there is no other that has a chance."

Wilcey agreed. "Leach courted her before she ran away to

kick up her heels on the stage," he said. "It looks like she won't say no any longer . . . not with Spearhead as a weddin' present."

"And another sure half million profit from sellin' land to the railroad," someone said enviously.

A hand tapped Bell's arm. The man was a saddle-warped old-time Spearhead cowpuncher called Latigo Jim. He drew Bell aside. "Buck Carmody's granddaughter sent me to find you," he murmured. "She wants a word with you in private. She's stayin' at the Mountain House. Front parlor room."

"Nancy Carmody?" Bell said unbelievingly. "What does she want?"

"I wouldn't know," Latigo Jim said. He was obviously hostile. It was plain that he shared the general opinion that the Minaret country would be better off without the presence of anyone named Enright.

Bell looked at the clock. He had two hours or more before the train was scheduled to pull out with his cattle. "You've got me curious," he said.

He walked to the Mountain House, climbed the stairs, and moved to the front. The door of the room opened before he could knock and the bulky, bronze-faced Jenny Walking Elk came marching sullenly into the hall. She gave him a suspicious and worried glance from her dark old eyes.

Nancy Carmody stood in the open door. "Come in, Mister Enright, please," she said. "Jenny and Latigo Jim do not approve of me, either, so don't feel that you're being discriminated against."

V

Nancy Carmody closed the door after he had stepped in. They were alone in a sitting room pleasantly furnished with a settee and brocaded chairs. A door to the right opened into a bedroom. A tray on a small table carried bottles of mineral water and decanters of spirits.

She motioned him toward the spindly-legged settee, then halted him, and stepped back a pace to inspect him from head to foot. "No, no," she said. "Not the sofa. Better take this chair. You're bigger than I realized, now that I can see you at close range."

Bell, instead, tested the settee, then gingerly sat on it. "I don't feel so penned in on this thing at least," he said.

"You have a mind of your own," she said approvingly, then moved to the table. "Sherry? Or would you prefer bourbon?"

"Neither at the moment, thanks," Bell said. He dangled his rain-soggy hat between his knees. He unfrogged his canvas jacket. He thought of the packets of money and hoped the bulges did not show.

Nancy Carmody poured sherry into a thimble-sized glass and seated herself facing him. She sipped the sherry. She had changed to a dark blue dress whose lines were simple but set off her figure to advantage.

She saw him eyeing the dress. "It flatters me," she said. "And because of that I paid more for it than I really should. In Paris."

Bell waited. Nancy Carmody was a surprisingly frank person. And also gorgeous. Her hair, in the lamplight, was a deep coppery shade. It was rich, healthy hair and her clear skin glowed with that same vital energy. She was firm-bosomed, and it was evident that she was well-endowed by Nature with all of womankind's allure.

She appraised him again, tilting her head from side to side. "I never dared look at you directly until today," she commented. "My, my, how afraid I was of you when I was a girl."

"Afraid?"

"Of course. Every time I encountered you on the trail, I expected something terrible to happen to me."

Bell said slowly: "I believe I savvy."

Her gaze did not waver. "I was taught that your father was the devil himself," she said. "And that you were just as bad. But I do not see any horns on you. Or a forked tail."

"I only spring 'em out on occasion," Bell said with a tight grin.

She placed the wine glass aside, and sat with her hands lying in her lap. They were slender hands, but seemed competently strong, with straight fingers and polished nails. "I know about your father's death," she said. "And about your being sent to prison and being pardoned."

Bell made no comment.

"You were convicted of harboring a fugitive from the law," Nancy went on. "You testified at your trial that you had no idea the man who came to your ranch was being pursued by a posse for robbing a bank in Marleyville. It was proved that he was an old-time outlaw who had once been a member of your father's Wild Bunch. His name was Tom Buell. But you said you thought he was only an old cowboy down on his luck. You were cooking him a meal when Pete Jennings and his posse showed up. Tom Buell was killed when he tried to resist arrest."

She again waited for him to speak. When he did not, she went on: "You were arrested and convicted and sentenced to five years in prison. You were pardoned by the governor only two months ago, but your father was dead . . . killed by someone who has never been identified."

"Why did you ask me to come here?" Bell said. "Not to tell me you are grown up now, and no longer afraid to face desperadoes like me?"

"I requested you to come here so that I could ask you to marry me," she said.

Bell blinked at her, startled. "Marry you?"

Nancy Carmody was cool and amused. "Yes. I'm proposing to you."

He started to rise impatiently. She halted him and became business-like. "Wait! This is a genuine offer. But the marriage I'm seeking is strictly a formality. A matter for the record. Marriage in name only to put it bluntly."

"I'm catching on," he said.

"That will make explanations easier," she said. "Do you mean by that that you've heard the conditions set down in my grandfather's will?"

"Yes."

"At Paddy O'Toole's saloon, I assume. I'm afraid that wasn't the first time my name has been mentioned in a saloon."

"The best people's names are mentioned in saloons," he said.

"And the other kind, also," she retorted lightly. "Even mine and yours. Now about my inheritance. Except for small bequests to Jenny Walking Elk and a few others, I am to receive all of Spearhead provided I marry a resident of Minaret Basin and settle down and be respectable. I must comply within thirty days or be disinherited."

Bell started to speak, but she halted him. "Before you accept or reject my fair hand," she said, and kept a stiff smile fixed on her lips, "make sure you understand me clearly. We will never actually be man and wife. The marriage will be dissolved at the first opportunity."

"You're aware that you're proposing fraud, aren't you?" he demanded.

"Legally, no," she responded. "Morally, yes. But who are we to quibble at the moral question if what they say about us is gospel? Let me say that I want to keep control of Spearhead in the hands of a Carmody. I have my reasons."

"Your reasons wouldn't have anything to do with the fact that the outfit is well worth hanging onto, now, would it?" Bell asked. "It's said to be worth half a million."

"Spearhead will be worth considerably more than that if the railroad builds out of the basin by way of the Clear Fork," she said. Some of the color had left her cheeks.

"So you've heard about that, too?" Bell said.

"Yes."

"If I agreed to marry you, what's in it for me?" he asked.

"Now there's a romantic thought," she murmured. "So tender, so considerate. What is your price, pray tell?"

"Don't you realize that, as your husband, I could just about write my own ticket?" Bell asked. "Husbands pack quite a lot of weight in this state."

"You could make trouble," she admitted.

"Why not Leach Valentine?" Bell demanded roughly. "They say he wants to marry you."

"Thank you for saying that," she said tartly. "It soothes my shattered vanity to know I am not repulsive in the eyes of some men at least."

"That's no answer," Bell stated.

"Perhaps I sent for you because you seem to be in need of money," she said. "Otherwise, you would not be trying to sell beef at this time of year."

Bell moved to the door. "It isn't every day a rich girl proposes to me. I'm a dunderhead for turning down such a chance."

"Is it because of Alice Drake that you're refusing me?"

Bell glared at her.

"I saw the way you were looking at her in Owen Randolph's office today," she added calmly. "And I happen to know that you've been in love with her since the both of you were children."

"Maybe that's one of the reasons," Bell said. "And maybe it's because I'm not sure this isn't some kind of a deadfall."

"I'll give you two thousand dollars," she said. "In cash. I'll make it twenty five hundred. No more. No less."

Bell swung around, came across the room, towering over her. "Why did you name that particular amount?" he snapped.

His vehemence startled her. "Why . . . why it seemed to me to be about the going price of temporary husbands," she stammered.

Bell grasped her arms, forced her to face him. "Exactly why did you pick me as a man who would go through with a thing like this?"

For the first time she was afraid of him. "Because . . . because we're looked upon as the same kind of people," she said, her voice suddenly bitter. "Because we're shunned here where we were raised. Because we're both . . . both wild ones!"

Bell's grip slackened, and his hands dropped away from her.

"There was another reason," she said slowly. "You Enrights, whatever else has been said about you, have a reputation for being men of your word."

"What you mean is that, if I went through this marriage ceremony, you could depend on me to take the money you offered, and never cause trouble for you again," he said.

Her voice rose a little, and he realized now how great was the strain she had been trying to conceal. "Yes! Yes . . . if that's the only answer you want, the only kind you can understand! Yes! Those are my reasons . . . and my terms. You'll be paid, and that will end the matter as far as you are concerned. You won't have to bruise your conscience by ever seeing me again after the ceremony. I'm quite sure I would not want to lay eyes on you again . . . ever!" The words were spilling from her furiously. "What right have you to question my motives? I told you that we're two of a kind. I'm the child of a dance-hall entertainer . . . a trollop, they say, who takes up with any man who meets my fancy." Tears were now streaming down her cheeks. "Well, you're Bell Enright, an ex-convict, the son of an outlaw! That's what they keep saying about you when your back is turned!"

Bell, gray-faced, opened the door.

"I'll ask no other man what I asked of you," she sobbed.

Bell went out, and closed the door. The sound of her grief followed him as he moved down the hall. Grim-faced, he descended the stairs and walked out of the Mountain House.

On the sidewalk he passed Owen Randolph, who was moving at his usual brisk military stride and swinging his walking stick. Owen said: "Oh, it's you, Bell. A raw evening with this wind."

VI

Owen entered the Mountain House. He paused inside the door and watched Bell walk away. Then he mounted the stairs and tapped on the door of Nancy Carmody's room.

She opened it and said, surprised: "Good evening, Mister Randolph."

"May I speak to you, my dear," Owen said. "And let's not be so formal. I want you to call me Owen."

In the room he laid his walking stick on the stand. "You've been crying!" he exclaimed. "Has anyone . . . ?"

"No," she said. "A good cry solves a lot of problems for a girl at times. Is it a business matter that brings you here? Has anything gone wrong?"

"On the contrary, everything may have gone exactly right," Owen responded heartily. "I want to talk to you about your grandfather's will. I feel he was unjust in making the stipulation. On the other hand, Spearhead is a huge ranch and a great responsibility for a young woman. Too great. It needs an experienced hand to guide it."

"Yes?" Nancy said wonderingly.

Owen took her hand. "I know of no other way than to speak out, my dear," he declared. "You need me. And not as a manager, heaven forbid, although you need me in that respect, also. But in other, nearer, and dearer ways. I have realized in the few hours since you returned home how happy I would be to have you as my wife."

"Your wife?" she almost screamed it. She snatched her hand from his grasp. "Why . . . why, that's ridic . . . that's impossible, Mister Randolph."

A tide of angry blood rushed into Owen's fine features. "Why impossible?" he demanded. "And you at first started to say such a thought was ridiculous."

A faint amusement now flickered in her gray eyes. "Let it stand as impossible," she said.

"If it's the difference in our ages, then you are being foolish," Owen snapped. "I'm in the prime of life. I do not believe my appearance is repulsive. I'm . . ."

Nancy began to laugh almost hysterically. "Good evening, Mister Randolph," she gasped between peals of amusement. "I believe you had better go now."

Owen was pale with anger. "After all, the name I offered you was at least respectable," he said.

He picked up his hat and stick, and walked out. After he had gone, Nancy stood in the room and looked at the closed door. All the laughter had died in her. And the laughter had not been laughter at all, in the first place, nor had it been directed at Owen Randolph. It had been a manifestation of her own view of herself.

She shivered a trifle as though some icy wind had touched her. She moved to the window and watched Owen cross the street and let himself into his office.

After leaving the Mountain House, Bell walked westward along Main Street. Darkness had come. Lamplight glowed in the town and a chill wind was pouring down from the snow fields of big Minaret.

Driven by the desires and the longings that were always in him, he walked as far as Buffalo Street and turned down this thoroughfare. Presently he came abreast of the Drake home. It was a comfortable, two-story clapboard house with a railed porch, a small front yard, and a low picket fence.

Lamplight glinted in the kitchen and he saw the shadows of Alice and her mother passing across the curtains as they completed the after-supper chores. He could visualize the content and warmth and the peace of mind in that house.

He rolled a cigarette and stood smoking it as he watched those shadows. It was good to put his own problems aside for a time.

Then he turned back to Main Street. The memory of Nancy Carmody's grief had been nagging at his thoughts and now it laid a heavy, depressing hand on him.

He passed a tall figure, standing out of the wind in the dark doorway on an empty street, and he was also smoking a cigarette.

" 'Evenin', Enright," Irons said.

"Turning gusty and bleak," Bell answered.

He walked on down the street, heading for the Nugget Restaurant. He was thinking that there was loneliness for Clay Irons, also, and times when he had only shadows upon which to pin his faith. Irons was a man who lived on trouble. Now he stood alone with his thoughts in a dark doorway on an empty street, listening to the same rumors of peace and well-being back of the same closed portals that Bell was passing.

Reaching a corner a block from the Nugget, a sudden gust of wind snatched Bell's hat from his head. He whirled, diving for it as it sailed low.

At the same instant a gun flamed from the darkness down the side street to his left. The bullet droned high above him and shattered a pane of glass in some upper window across the street. He instinctively sprawled flat on the muddy walk and lay there, hearing the jangle of falling glass.

No other shot came. Doors began to open. Someone came along the street at a run. It was Clay Irons.

Bell wriggled to the building wall, drew himself along and around the corner, before he risked rising to his feet.

Irons reached him, then, a pistol in his hand and said: "It's you, Enright? Are you hit?"

"No," Bell said, and explained what had happened.

He and Irons moved cautiously down the side street. 100 feet from the corner a heavy freighting dray stood flanking the sidewalk, left there by its teamster owner for the night. Beyond that was a muddy alley that paralleled Main Street, east and west. Farther along were a blacksmith shop, a wood yard, and feed store, and then the dreary fringe of the railroad yards. There was no sign of any human presence.

Pete Jennings arrived with several other curious citizens. Jennings listened to Bell's story. "And you've got no idea who did it?" the deputy asked scoffingly.

Bell knew then that Jennings believed this shooting had its roots in some of the same outlaw feuds that he believed were responsible for Josh Enright's murder. The deputy took the view that such grudges were better settled among the principals and that it would be a public benefit if all concerned were eliminated.

Still, at Irons's insistence, Jennings searched the vicinity. It proved to be a waste of time.

Leach Valentine and Shep Murdock had joined the bystanders. "Looks like you'll live to be shot at another day," Valentine said to Bell.

He and Bell had clashed in the past, and had traded punches on one occasion at roundup before Buck Carmody had separated them.

"After this," Valentine went on, "it'd be better if you stood where no women might be in the line of fire, fellow. That bullet might have killed Nancy Carmody. It broke the window in her hotel room and smashed into the ceiling."

Bell had not realized that the falling glass had come from the Mountain House.

"Mebbe you're givin' Enright ideas, Leach," said Shep Murdock, his thick lips grinning. "Maybe he'll figure it'll be safer to stand near women an' kids from now on. Petticoats sometimes make a man bulletproof. Then this country might never git rid o' him."

Bell placed the heel of his hand against Shep Murdock's underslung jaw and shoved the man violently against a wall. "Tell that to the petticoats," he said.

Murdock came bouncing off the wall with all the fury and purpose of a tough man sure of his prowess. He said: "You damned jailbird, I'll . . ."

Irons stepped quickly between them. "You baited him into it, Murdock," he said. "What did you think he'd do? Stand like a lamb and let you shear him with your insults?"

"Stay out of this, Irons," Leach Valentine snapped. "Enright laid hands on him. Shep's entitled to satisfaction."

Irons looked at Pete Jennings. "This is your town, Pete," he said.

Jennings swung on his heel and walked away without a word. He didn't intend to interfere.

Murdock laughed, and pulled off his baggy saddle coat and unbuckled his gun belt.

Other bystanders now suddenly had business elsewhere.

Irons sighed. "All right. I can see this didn't start tonight, did it? You might as well settle it. But keep it down to fists. No gun play. Enright isn't armed."

"You're acting like you're the law here instead of Pete,"

Valentine said. "You don't weigh that many tons, Irons."

Irons said nothing. Bell pulled off his coat, and handed it to him. "I've got a couple of dollars in it that I can't afford to lose," he said.

Murdock came at him then. He was tough and built for rough going. He swung both fists in short trip-hammer punches, bulled his head aside in an attempt to shatter teeth and jaw bone, and kicked savagely as he moved in and out.

Bell took punishment—and dealt it out. Murdock's greater weight told at first. Bell was slammed against a building wall by Murdock's rush and a fist that was shockingly heavy found his body. He came up inside Murdock's clubbing arms, driving both fists upward in short uppercuts to the chin. Murdock's head rocked back, and he momentarily retreated.

Bell slid away from him again, and drove a fist to the man's short ribs. Murdock whirled with amazing agility and, even though he was hurt by that punch, slammed an elbow into Bell's throat. Bell staggered backward, gagging for breath, and Murdock caught him with a solid smash to the jaw.

Badly hurt, Bell went down. Murdock moved in, then leaped high, intending to drive his boot heels into his victim's face, but Bell rolled aside in time. He caught both of the man's heavy ankles, heaved himself to his feet, and brought his quarry down on the sidewalk on the flat of his back with breath-taking impact.

Even so Murdock scrambled back to his feet. He was wheezing, blood dripping from his battered face.

Bell was in little better shape, but he sensed that fear had now crawled into Murdock's mind. And uncertainty. Up to this moment Murdock had been confident that his greater weight and strength would prevail.

Bell forced himself to renew the attack. He took a smash to the face, and another to the body, but Murdock's strength was fading. The man swayed off balance, and Bell pumped a right to the heart and a left to the point of the chin. Murdock staggered back, tried to brace himself. But his knees quivered and he reeled drunkenly. Bell followed him, drove another punch to the body. Murdock skidded against a building wall. His feet slid out, and he sat down heavily, then slumped sideways, lying in a limp, twisted heap.

Bell caught a tie rail and fought to pull some air into his laboring lungs. Dimly he heard Irons's crisp voice speaking. "You were lucky, Valentine. It might have been you that got caught in the wringer."

Owen Randolph arrived, his features flushed and perturbed. "Bell, confound it . . . ," he said helplessly. "More brawling."

Someone brought water and Valentine angrily poured it on Murdock. He got his man to his feet finally, and led him away.

"First a fight with Sim Gillis, then a shooting, and now another fight," Owen said. "There isn't much more help I can give you, Bell." And he, too, walked away, his whole bearing stiff and reproachful.

Bell now became aware of the punishment he had taken. He tested various areas of his body with probing fingers. "Nothing broken as far as I can make out," he observed.

"You fought like a man who couldn't afford to lose," Irons remarked. "Like you had a sight more at stake than he did. Heaven spare me from bumpin' into a dedicated man. An' what did Murdock have to fight about? What was his grudge?"

"He and Valentine were with Pete Jennings the night I was arrested," Bell said. "Jennings had deputized them. We Enrights had locked horns with them a couple of times before at roundups when they tried to crowd us. We made them back down one time right in front of Buck Carmody when they hinted that we were stealing cattle. Buck Carmody fired Murdock and he never got back on the Spearhead payroll until Valentine hired him a couple months ago."

"I begin to see that you gentlemen have reason for not admirin' each other," Irons observed.

"They tried to take it out on me the night they helped Jennings arrest me." Bell shrugged. "I hit Valentine with my handcuffs an' knocked him out, and kicked Murdock in the belly. Then somebody belted me with a gun muzzle. I woke up in jail, but they had worked me over when I was out."

"Come on," Irons said. "I've got a room at the Mountain House. We better take a peek at you to make sure it's only bruises an' cuts you picked up."

VII

Entering the hotel, Bell and Irons ascended the stairs. "Just a moment," Bell said. He moved toward the door of the rooms Nancy Carmody occupied. But it opened before he could knock.

She stood there, with Jenny Walking Elk peering anxiously from the background. "I've been expecting you," she said. "We seem to have been somewhat in the path of the same bullet. Come in."

She ushered him and Irons into the sitting room.

"I'm happy you weren't hurt," Bell said.

"Oh, there was no chance of that," she said. "I wasn't even in this room. I had gone into the bedroom."

The bullet had shattered the pane in the upper sash of a front window and had pierced the shade and the chintz curtain. The broken glass had been removed and a piece of cloth had been tacked over the opening.

Irons stood on a chair and located the spot where the slug was buried in the ceiling. He produced a pocket knife, and, after some effort, dug the battered bullet from the lath in which it was embedded beneath the plaster.

They turned to leave. Nancy halted Bell. "I saw the fight,"

she said. "Your face needs attention. Do you have any other injuries?"

"Nothing that's more than skin deep," he said. "I'm in sort of a hurry."

"This won't take long," she assured him.

"Entirely unnecessary," Bell said.

"Pull off your coat and shirt," Nancy said. "Wait . . . I'll help you. Jenny, give me a hand."

"I don't want any fuss, and . . . ," Bell began.

But they were upon him. Jenny Walking Elk sniffed scornfully. "Raise arms!" she commanded. Resistance was too painful, and, before Bell could escape, they had him stripped to the waist.

Jenny Walking Elk pointed to livid bruises on his ribs and uttered a cackling laugh. "She has a keen sense of humor," Bell commented sourly. "She must have fun at a funeral."

Nancy used arnica and lotion and applied court plaster. "There may be a scar from that one on the cheek bone," she commented. "It'll give you a distinguished appearance."

Bell thanked them, and donned his shirt and coat. Irons accepted a brandy Nancy poured. "Your very good health, miss," he said, bowing gallantly. "It is my belief Spearhead will have an owner of which it can be proud."

"I haven't found me a husband yet," she said. "I've had an offer, however."

"Leach Valentine," Bell said, stating it as a fact.

She started to speak and tell them about Owen Randolph's proposal, then decided there was no point in it. "I've also been refused once already," she said.

"Refused?" Irons said incredulously. "Why the varmint ought to be thrashed. Fair lady, may I have the honor of askin' your hand in marriage?"

"I'll add your name to the list of candidates," she said. "Do you smoke or drink, and are you kind to children and old ladies?"

"I reckon that let's me out," Irons said gloomily. "I could give up 'most anythin' except pushin' old ladies in the mud once in a while."

He and Bell left then. Emerging from the Mountain House, they headed for the Nugget Restaurant. "So she asked you to marry her?" Irons spoke quietly. "And you turned her down?"

Bell glared at him.

"Take it easy," Irons said. "I only guessed it."

They entered the eating house, and Bell led the way to a table which was shielded from observation through any of the windows. "You're smartin' up," Irons commented. "A man soon learns to be spooky after he's been shot at."

"Did it occur to you that you could have been the person who did the shooting?" Bell asked.

Irons sat motionlessly a moment. "An' do you really think it was me?" he countered.

They measured each other. Then Bell shook his head. "No. And that bullet wasn't fired at me. You know that as well as I do."

The tension faded. Irons nodded. "I marked the angle of fire just as you did. The shot came from someone hunkered back o' that dray on the side street. From that position all he could see was the window of the rooms Nancy Carmody was occupyin'. You just naturally happened to step around that corner as this fella cut loose. The bullet went high over your head."

"It wasn't meant to kill me, and certainly not her," Bell said. "At least, that's the way it stacks up. Then why was it fired?"

"It could have been the work of a drunken man or someone who figured they didn't get a fair shake in Buck Carmody's will," Irons said. "Or it might have been done to intimidate her for some reason."

They ordered food. When the waitress had gone back to the kitchen, Irons spoke again. "If that shot had really been fired at you, you'd maybe have had a reason for puttin' me on your list of suspects. I might have a motive."

"Motive?"

"Alice Drake is a mighty sweet girl," Irons said slowly. "I met her the first summer the Mid C built into the basin. Fact is I courted her right ardent. But she never could forget that I was Clay Irons who always packed guns on his hip an' always made sure nobody could sneak up on him, just like we're sittin' now. For she's a gentle person, Enright. I don't want to see her hurt. I wouldn't take kindly to watchin' her heart get broken by marryin' with the wrong man."

"With a wild one, you mean," Bell said. "Like me."

VIII

Owen Randolph, after he had left the scene of Bell's fight with Shep Murdock, walked up the street and finally paused in the doorway of his office. He watched Valentine lead the groggy Murdock into the Crystal Bar. Presently Valentine emerged.

Owen strolled farther up the street and waited for Valentine in the dark doorway of the same tin shop that had sheltered Clay Irons earlier.

Cold rage quivered in Owen's voice when Valentine reached his side. "Quit this damned drinking, Leach. You and that other sot could have ruined everything by starting that brawl."

Valentine took his time answering. He rolled a cigarette, lighted it, and casually snuffed the match. His acquaintanceship with Owen Randolph dated back to before Tamarack. They had first met when Owen had acted as Valentine's attorney in a cattle-stealing case in Nevada. Owen had failed to win an acquittal for Valentine, but had been more successful at smuggling a hacksaw and a gun into the cell with which Valentine escaped from the small cow town jail during the night.

Later on they had been associated in a shake-down and claim-jumping enterprise in South Dakota. The scheme was for Owen to seek a flaw, or a pretended flaw, in a homesteader's papers. Then Valentine would milk the victim for what he could pay, or jump the claim and settle some new land seeker on the property—for a fee.

Finally both of them were forced to flee Dakota between suns to escape a band of night-riding men who carried tar and feathers as well as hang ropes. They had gone separate ways until chance had brought them together again here at Tamarack. Now they were in partnership once more. But there was neither affection nor respect between them.

"Enright pushed Shep in the face," Valentine finally said. "After that there was no stopping it."

"You could have stopped it, but you wanted it to go on," Owen snapped. "You hoped Murdock would do a job you're not sure you can handle yourself."

Valentine laughed jeeringly. "I don't go in for rolling in the mud. When I take out after our friend from the Boiling Fork, it'll be with a gun. But you tried to beat me to it tonight, Owen. You could have spoiled things yourself by being caught when you took that shot at him."

"Don't be an idiot!" Owen snapped. "I didn't shoot at him!"

"No?" Valentine was surprised. "If you weren't the one, then who . . . ?" He broke off. It had occurred to him that Owen had not directly denied firing the shot. He might have only been side-stepping a direct answer.

"I trust you've taken care of the matter we discussed so lengthily this afternoon, Leach?" Owen said ominously.

"Right after dark." Valentine nodded. "Shep did it. He worked as a brakeman in the past, so he knew how to handle it. Those cattle cars are old style and so is the caboose. Hand brakes only. He jammed them with spikes."

"And I suppose you stayed warm and cozy in some saloon and have taken Murdock's word for it," Owen said. "Leach, I want no slip-up on this! It's a heaven-sent chance to put E Loop in such a financial hole there can't be any question about my right to take it over. I prefer that you ride that train. Let Murdock be the one who takes the horses to Summit. And make sure both of you slip away unnoticed."

"You treat me like a child, Owen!" Valentine raged. "Shep is experienced at railroading. I'm not. He can handle things on the train. I'll pick him up at the siding."

"I wish you were a child," Owen said. "Then I could overlook your weaknesses. But you're not. You never fooled me. I wonder if you'll fool Nancy Carmody." He paused and presently added reflectively, as though trying to push down his own doubts: "Well, she'll have to marry you by default, at least. She has no choice."

"I still say this marriage was an idiotic mistake," Valentine grated. "Oh, I'll marry her. And it won't be by default. I've never seen a woman I couldn't have if I set my mind to it. But it only complicates things. Why didn't you just cut her off with a dollar as everybody expected Buck Carmody to do?"

"I explained that," Owen said with the air of one addressing a mental inferior. "Nancy is the only kin. As such she could legally attack a disinheritance and that would bring an examination of the will into open court. We must avoid that at all costs. To all intents and purposes she now inherits everything. The stipulation that she marry is characteristic of Buck Carmody. I'm sure this, above everything else, will avert any suspicion in regard to the will."

"It's riding twice around the corral to reach the gate," Valentine grumbled. "It'd have been better to have willed it all to this fake charity set-up of yours. With you and me as trustees we'd have milked the cow just as easy."

"But not as thoroughly," Owen said impatiently. "Our profit would have been much smaller, for it would have been a case of slow liquidation. And we would always have been in danger of an embezzlement charge if we made the slightest error."

"I can still see a lot of snags," Valentine said.

"She'll have to marry you," Owen said. "After all, outwardly, you are a dashing and handsome man with a future. Any girl with the reputation she has would be a fool to look any further. Nancy Carmody is no fool. She has no other choice." He tolled off his points as though schooling a dull pupil. "We'll start selling off lots in a landsite on the Clear Fork within twenty-four hours after the wedding. I've already had it secretly surveyed. We've got to move fast and cash in before any announcement comes from Mid C. We should make a fortune in a month's time. By then I'll own Bell Enright's place. And by that time the weather will be settled and the cat will be out of the bag. We'll make another hundred thousand."

"Someday folks are going to add two and two together," Valentine said uneasily.

"There can be no gain without risks." Owen shrugged.

"What about Nancy? You act as though she won't even exist after I marry her. After all, Spearhead will be in her name."

"Blast it all, Leach!" Owen exploded. "You'll be the lord in that manor. All a woman wants is affection, fine clothes, and babies. I'm sure you'll find time to confer these on her. There'll be money enough, I assure you, for that and for whatever other pleasures you might seek on the side." Owen paused and looked at his watch. "It's time you were moving," he said.

Valentine studied the hot tip of his cigarette a moment. "If this thing works," he murmured, "the caboose will go along with the cattle cars. There'll be a couple of trainmen in that caboose with Enright."

Owen did not answer. There was no change in his expression as he tucked his walking stick under his arm and regarded the other man with quizzical coolness.

"You're a cold fish, Owen," Valentine said. Then he walked off down the street.

He entered the Crystal Bar where Shep Murdock, court plaster on his jaw, stood tasting a drink and wincing as the alcohol stung his bruised and swollen lips.

Their glances met briefly. They left the place some five minutes apart. Valentine made his way alone to where two saddle horses were tied among the deserted cattle pens near the railroad track south of the depot. He mounted, and rode away along the tracks, leading the other horse. He headed for the Clear Fork wagon bridge on the road to Summit, but he stayed off the trail for he did not wish to be seen.

Owen Randolph remained standing in that dark doorway in Tamarack for a considerable time. He watched Bell and Irons emerge from the Mountain House and walk to the Nugget.

The day had started well enough for his plans, with the arrival of Nancy and the reading of the will. Apparently she had accepted the provisions in the document unquestioningly. Then had come the snags. The first was the discovery of the existence of a person named Matt Barker. Owen had never before heard of this man, but suddenly it had become a matter of his own survival or Barker's.

The second complication was Nancy herself. She had been a headstrong, wild-riding girl of fifteen when he had first worked his way into an acquaintanceship and into the confidence of her grandfather. He had regarded her as a rattle-brained child of limited intelligence.

Later on, he was startled to find that the child to whom he had paid so little heed had blossomed into a vividly handsome and shapely young woman who was educated and trained to preside over the social affairs at Spearhead. Leach Valentine had arrived in Minaret Basin by that time, and had at once begun courting the girl who was not only stunningly pretty, but was heiress apparent to the mighty Spearhead.

Then she had fled from Spearhead out of reach of both of them. Owen had been sure of his ability to handle her when she returned for the reading of Buck Carmody's will. It had been his conviction that beauty never went hand-in-hand with real intelligence. Now he was not so sure. He had expected to find her conceited, vain—and shallow. Instead, he had been confronted by a poised, young woman who was not only breathtakingly feminine, but was also endowed with a keen, discerning mind.

A doubt had come to him that Valentine would sweep her off her feet as easily as he had taken for granted. And the truth was that Owen had suddenly found himself wanting Nancy Carmody for himself.

The news that Matt Barker was dickering with Bell for a chance to talk had driven him almost into a panic. And it had shaken Valentine and Murdock. Then had come his own ignominious retreat from Nancy's presence after her rejection of his marriage offer. He had been in a wild rage at that moment— the unreasoning anger of a scorned man in whom pride and vanity burned like a bright flame. For one of the few times in his life he had let emotion gain the upper hand. He had left his office by the rear door, made his way to the dark side street, and had crouched back of that dray with murder in his mind, watching the windows of the rooms Nancy occupied. Then a measure of sanity had returned and he had remembered that her death would spoil his own plans. But he could not restrain himself from firing a bullet through the window—a petty and dangerous display of temper, he now conceded.

In the nearby railroad yards a train whistle sounded three blasts. He saw Bell go hurrying past on Main Street, heading for the yards. Number 17, the night train to Marleyville, was making ready to pull out.

Owen strolled to the depot, and stood in the shadows. Presently the engine came chuffing from the yards, dragging a string of cars. At the end of the line were the cattle cars carrying Bell's steers.

Then the caboose came clanking abreast. In the lighted interior Owen could see Bell pulling off his saddle coat. Owen remained motionless until the running lights of the caboose had vanished down the track. Then, his face impassive, he strolled away.

Inside the caboose, Bell hung his jacket on a nail. The interior was heated by a wood stove. Johnson, the brakeman, was on watch in the cupola, only his legs visible, and Pat McGonigle, the conductor, was mumbling to himself as he thumbed through a sheaf of papers clipped to a board.

Bell spread his blanket on one of the narrow benches and stretched out. He lay down, relaxing his tired muscles while he recalled the day's amazing developments. He thought of Alice and the faith she had shown in him when she had asked him to squire her to the sociable. And he wondered what her reaction would be if she knew he was now on his way to attempt to buy the escape from jail of a man accused of murder. He also thought of Nancy Carmody and her offer of marriage and the memory brought a silent, derisive laughter to him.

The train churned laboriously up the curving grade to the bench and picked up speed. Soon Bell heard the rumble of the wheels as the train crossed the Clear Fork bridge. Looking out, he saw that a half moon was breaking through the clouds. In its light that river appeared wild and untrammeled beneath the bridge.

The train lurched into the sharp curve beyond the bridge and Bell was propelled against the wall by centrifugal force, for the engineer was making all the speed he could muster as he drove his load at the mile-long climb to Summit.

The train straightened and the speed began to fade on the climb. He could hear the laboring exhaust of the engine. The two trainmen were straining with the engine, for there were times when the train was unable to make the Summit grade. That meant double hauling and extra work.

Suddenly progress slowed to a full halt. Bell looked out and saw that they were near the crest. McGonigle burst into a rage. "Bad cess to thim cursed cattle he wishes on us!" he yelled. "We're stalled, an' this means . . ."

They became aware of motion again—motion that increased perceptibly, but in the wrong direction.

"We're going backward!" Bell yelled.

He leaped to the door, tore it open, and hung from a hand rail, peering ahead. "We've broken loose!" he shouted. "We're running away, down the grade!"

McGonigle had already leaped to the hand brake on the caboose and was attempting to twist the iron wheel. "Holy Mother!" the man screeched, his face suddenly ashen. "The brake won't take hold! 'Tis jammed, it is!"

Bell frantically leaped to the swaying ladder that ascended to the roof of the first cattle car, and mounted. He knew Johnson was following.

Reaching the top, the wind struck him with savage force and he realized that they were in desperate trouble. The runaway cars were picking up velocity each second, and had already attained a swaying speed that made foot progress a matter of heart-stopping peril.

He crouched and fought his way along the reeling runway. Darkness was an enemy, upsetting his sense of equilibrium.

Once he lost his balance and staggered off the runway and toward the blackness beyond the combing of the swaying car. He threw himself flat, clawing wildly for hand hold. His legs swung into the clear and he would have gone hurtling from the train, except that his right hand found a broken board in the roof at the last instant, and this gave him a firm enough grip to check his slide.

With ice in the pit of his stomach he drew himself back to safety. Johnson, crawling along the runway, on hands and knees, reached the hand brake on the first car.

Bell regained the runway, made his way past Johnson, and crawled along the second car to the iron wheel. He twisted it frantically. It turned once, then stopped. He heard a hoarse shout of despair from Johnson.

"This brake is jammed, too!" the man screeched. "Gawd! We'll go into the river!"

Bell now remembered the sweeping curve on the brink of the torrential Clear Fork at the foot of the long slant.

McGonigle's strident voice, muffled by the *clatter* of the train, reached them from the caboose. "Sure an' it's hopeless! Jump, ye fools, before it's too late!"

The wind was a wild banshee wail in the night, threatening to pluck both Bell and Johnson from the tops of the cars. "I'm leavin'!" Johnson howled, and disappeared between cars.

Bell slid down the nearest ladder between the two swaying cars. The high whine of the wheels steadily building up speed was in his ears. At the same time he heard the cattle moaning piteously—as if they sensed that their doom was at hand. These were his cattle—and they were being snatched from him. There was no way of saving them.

He caught a hand rail and swung out from the car, a foot on the thin iron support. The white shadow of snowbanks were spinning past, promising a faint hope of survival.

He caught a glimpse of McGonigle leaping from the step of the caboose. Then Johnson left the doomed train and went sailing into the darkness. Bell poised and followed.

He struck the white snowbank and went tumbling end over end like a toy thrown by a child. The snow was old, beaten and softened on the surface by the rain, but crusted underneath from thaws and freezes. Below that it was still soft and white as down. He broke through this crust and the cushioning virgin snow beneath saved him.

He lay there, jarred to the marrow for a time, his head ringing. Finally he sat up. The wailing of the locomotive whistle sounded. The remainder of the train had come to a stop on the level summit only a few hundred yards away.

Receding down the grade, gathering greater speed, were his cattle in their cars, and the lighted caboose. Then they vanished into the distance and the darkness. Moments later a hollow, crashing sound that was sustained for an agonizing moment—like the offense of a discord struck on strings—filled the night. Afterward, there was a dread, agonizing silence.

Bell discovered that he had no broken bones, but he knew he had suffered new bruises, and that his left eye was swelling. His shirt was torn to shreds and his trousers were in little better shape. The heels of both boots had been wrenched off. Scouring around in the darkness, he finally found McGonigle and Johnson. The latter was groaning and clutching a broken leg. McGonigle lay unconscious against a boulder in the ditch.

The remainder of the train crew now came running down the track. Bell left the two injured men in their care and ran in long, straining strides down the grade.

It was a brutal mile in the darkness. He at last reached the curve that led into the approach to the bridge. Here the rails were ripped up and he saw a deep, fresh gouge on the shoulder of the roadbed.

Presently the moon emerged from the wind-whipped clouds, revealing the wheel truck of one of the cattle cars speared on a large boulder at the margin of the river. There was nothing else.

It was then he remembered that not only were his cattle gone, but also his saddle coat with the $2,500 he had borrowed from Owen Randolph.

IX

It was well past midnight before a yard engine steamed out from Tamarack, pushing flat cars and a bunk car filled with men and equipment. Clay Irons swung down from the engine and came striding to meet Bell who stood in the beam cast by the headlight. It was raining again—another cold, driving downpour as bleak as Bell's thoughts.

Irons was wrapped in a yellow slicker that flapped about his long legs. Bell was alone. The forward section of the train had proceeded to Marleyville soon after the wreck in order to speed the injured men to a hospital. At Irons's heels were other railroad men and also Wilcey Pickens. Wilcey came to Bell's side, placed a hand on his arm. He stood listening to the roar of the nearby river. "Holy mighty," he said glumly. "Fifty-seven head o' stock gone in one flicker."

"Sorry we were so long," Irons said. "We got the first rumble of this from the dispatcher at Marleyville after the front end pulled in there. It took time to get a crew."

"How's McGonigle?" Bell asked.

"Dead," Irons said. "He died as they were pullin' into Marleyville."

"Johnson?"

"He'll make it." Irons peered closely at Bell. "You didn't get off easy either from the looks of you."

"Clothes and skin ripped and other things I'll likely find out about tomorrow," Bell said.

Irons now realized that Bell was without coat and almost shirtless in the bitter rain. He sent men hurrying, and they returned with borrowed garments and shoes.

"Tell me about it," Irons said.

Bell related what he knew. "McGonigle yelled that he was having trouble with the hand brake," he concluded. "So was I, and I think Johnson was, also. By that time it was too late to do anything but jump. Everything else went into the river."

Irons looked incredulously at the torrent. "Everything?"

"I tried to hunt downstream, but it was too dark and hell on a man without heels on his boots," Bell said.

At dawn he and Irons and Wilcey and two of Irons's men from the Mid C started downstream on foot, scanning the shorelines. After a time they began sighting carcasses of drowned steers wedged in driftwood or caught in the brush in backwater.

Bell suddenly broke into a run. A red-painted object was afloat in willow brush and cottonwoods in a marsh that the rising river was invading. "The caboose!" he panted. He waded waist deep into the water to reach it. He was breathing hard. Then the eddying current swung the object around so that he and Irons and others all had a view.

What he had found was only a portion of the caboose. The car had been ripped apart and its contents had been scattered in the river. Bell had hoped he would find the car intact, with his saddle coat still trapped inside. The greenbacks would have been redeemable even though water-soaked.

He came wading out of the water and sat down and emptied the borrowed shoes. He knew now the coat and the money were somewhere at the bottom of the river. He was beat out and gray-faced.

"The railroad is liable," Irons said. "Mid C will pay."

Bell said: "Sure." Such a procedure would take weeks,

perhaps months. By that time it would be too late to help Matt Barker. In any event there would be no restitution of the money. He could not even reveal its loss. To do so would mean explanation.

He crowded his feet into the wet shoes again. "How soon can I get back to Tamarack?" he asked.

"Right away," Irons said. "I'll send you in on the engine." He turned to the others. "Keep lookin'. Fetch anything you find to me personal."

He and Bell walked upriver to the bridge.

"From the way you acted I got the idea there had been somethin' of 'special value to you in the caboose," Irons finally remarked.

"Some old keepsakes in my coat," Bell said.

Irons knew that wasn't the right answer, but he asked no further questions. The work crew was making headway at repairing the gap in the rails. "We ought to have it cleaned up in about an hour or so," the foreman said.

Irons beckoned to the engineer to join them. "You're to run into town, Ed," he said. "Enright is ridin' in with you. As soon as you hit, get hold of Fred Wyatt an' tell him to hire half a dozen good saddle horses at the livery, load 'em into anything he's got handy, an' fetch 'em out here on your way back. Bring along planks or a stage so we can unload 'em out here."

"Saddle horses," the engineer marveled. "Now what would you want with . . . ?"

"I want 'em right quick," Irons said, and there was a sudden lash of authority in his tone that sent the man hurrying to climb into his cab.

Bell boarded the engine and stood in the warmth of the boiler head as it backed across the bridge and dropped down the bench toward Tamarack.

"Horses," the engineer grumbled. "What'n blue blazes would

Irons want with saddle horses on a day like this? You git the daw-gonedest errands to run when you're a hogger on the Mid C."

Bell sat wearily on the fireman's bench. That individual eyed him and said: "Man, you've been through the grinder. That moused eye is a beaut."

Bell knew that he must look like the wrath of heaven. The coat Irons had found for him was tight at the shoulders and short in the sleeves. His unshaven face was pinched with cold and fatigue and carried a new crop of bruises and patches of dried blood. His hair was matted by rain and blood and grit. And he had lost a precious day's time. He had only one more day of grace if he were to buy Matt Barker's release.

A sensible man, he reflected, would back out before it was too late. He had gambled $2,500 already on a vague and tenuous possibility and lost. And he was now hopelessly in debt to Owen. On top of that it was a desperate and lawless venture at best, and he was risking more than money if anything went wrong. He was gambling with his freedom and perhaps even his life.

Owen might be right in saying that Barker had only invented that story about being an eyewitness to Josh Enright's murder in order to dupe Bell. Still, he was the one who had talked to Barker personally, not Owen. He had questioned and cross-questioned Barker. The man was not obtuse or particularly sharp-witted. Bell was certain he was telling the truth. He was sure his father's death was not the fruit of some old feud from outlaw days. Those days had been far behind for Josh Enright. He had scrupulously adhered to the promises he had made when he was pardoned and had never again overstepped the law. He had not found this easy. There had been no helping hands for a man of his reputation.

Bell's mother had been only sixteen when she had married

Josh Enright. It was she who had induced him to make his peace with the law and accept the penalty. Bell had been eight years of age when his father was pardoned. Josh Enright had finally settled on the Boiling Fork. It was an area he knew well. It was wild and remote and had, in fact, been the hide-out for the Enright Wild Bunch. There Bell's mother had died when he was twelve and there he and his father had lived, scorned by their neighbors. Other outfits in the Minaret, like Spearhead, had prospered mightily. But E Loop had not prospered. E Loop cattle had always been regarded as fair game for neighboring outfits in need of beef for their tables.

Bell had always felt that his father had been shot by someone he had no reason to distrust, for the bullet had been fired at such close range that powder flame had deeply scorched the coat. Barker's version bore this out. If Barker was telling the truth, two men were involved.

The engine clattered over switch frogs in the Tamarack yards, arousing him. The decision could be put off no longer. If he were to go through with it, he needed $2,500 more. There was Owen Randolph, of course. Owen would probably advance the money, but he was sure to regard it as throwing good cash after bad. And it meant giving up any last hope of holding onto E Loop. But there was still Nancy Carmody, and her offer of marriage.

Bell alighted at the depot and walked up Main Street. Two Spearhead saddle horses stood at the rail in front of the Mountain House along with a two-seated surrey with a team in harness. The rig belonged to Spearhead and Latigo Jim sat waiting in the driver's seat, wrapped in a lap robe. The two saddle mounts wore Spearhead brands, also.

Through the window he now saw Leach Valentine and Shep Murdock in the hotel eating room, coffee mugs before them and cigarette smoke rising. They did not see him as he entered by way of the clerk's office and climbed the stairs.

He tapped on the door of Nancy Carmody's room. It was opened by Jenny Walking Elk. Before Bell could speak, she slammed the portal in his face.

But he heard the sound of brisk heels come from the bedroom and Nancy's voice said: "Jenny, what are you trying to do?"

The door opened again, and she stood there, a startled expression rising into her eyes. Bell had forgotten his appearance. Now he became acutely conscious of it.

"Not another fist fight?" she said.

"I'd like to talk to you," Bell said. "Alone."

She inspected him with her gray eyes, and then color swiftly moved up from her throat. He knew that she suddenly understood why he had come here. She stood appraising him, as though trying to estimate her course. For a moment he thought she had decided, also, to close the door in his face.

Then she seemed to reach some conclusion. She said, her voice very low: "Come in."

Bell entered. Nancy turned to Jenny Walking Elk. "Wait for me downstairs, Jen-Jen."

But she had to push almost forcibly the frowning Indian woman through the door.

She closed it and tried to draw a smile to her lips. It was a thin failure. "Jenny only wants to see that I make no mistakes," she explained.

"Then maybe you'd better bring her back," Bell said.

"I prefer to be responsible for my own errors," she said.

"Is the matter we talked over yesterday still open to discussion?" he asked shakily.

The color was higher than ever in her now. But it was a hot and resentful anger. "You're referring to my proposal of marriage, of course."

"If your offer still stands, then it's all right with me," Bell said lamely.

"Am I to understand that you are agreeing to our betrothal?" she asked, her voice very brittle.

"Yes," Bell said, and felt the deep thrust of her resentment. "I'd get down on my knees if that would please you, but I'm too damned stiff and sore."

"How gallant! How tender and devoted you are. How romantic and chivalrous."

Bell looked down at himself. He said wryly. "I'm not much for appearances, ma'am. But I'm true blue. Black and blue, in fact."

That melted some of Nancy's bitterness. In spite of herself she was forced to laugh a little. "You at least know how to unbend me when I go stiff-necked with pride," she said. "You're not exactly the picture of a dashing bridegroom every girl envisions when she stocks her hope chest, but I admit that, after all, I must not look a gift horse in the mouth. Whatever happened to you?"

"Just a railroad wreck this time," Bell said.

"You're joking!"

Bell told her briefly of the disaster on Summit grade. All her laughter was gone. "Oh, I'm sorry," she breathed.

"You told me you would pay twenty-five hundred dollars," Bell said slowly. "I need the money. How soon could you raise it . . . in cash?"

"How soon do you want it?"

"Today, if possible."

"Today?" She was astonished. She started another question, then decided against it. "My grandfather had a friend who is head of a bank in Marleyville," she said after a time. "Bill Sutton. I'm sure he'll loan the money to me. But I'll have to go to Marleyville personally."

"Won't Owen Randolph lend it to you?"

"I prefer that Mister Randolph know nothing about my marriage until it's an accomplished fact," she said.

"You figure he'd disapprove," Bell observed. "He might argue you into believing you could do better."

"I want to surprise him," she said.

"He'll be surprised," Bell said. "That's for sure."

"There's a morning train to Marleyville, I believe," she said. "I'll go there today and see Bill Sutton, if it's really that urgent."

"They'll have the track open soon," Bell said. "The train will be late pulling out, but it still should be in Marleyville on time. I'll go with you. That will speed things up. We can get the license there and go through the ceremony before a justice of peace in short order."

The warm color had receded from her. There was no animation in her now. "You mean, of course, as soon as the money is in your hands," she said. "This is marriage on a cash basis."

"It was understood that this was to be only a formality," Bell said slowly.

"It will be a mockery of a sacred contract," she said. "Will you kiss the bride, or can I expect just a written receipt, acknowledging payment in full?"

"I get twenty-five hundred dollars, but you get Spearhead out of this mockery," Bell said.

That hurt. He saw her catch her small underlip in her teeth. She sat silently for a time. "What will you say to Alice Drake?" she finally asked.

It was his turn to wince a trifle. "She'll understand," he said. "She'll understand when I tell her about the devils that drive me." Then he added hastily: "Forget that. I'm driven by nobody."

Her expression changed. "Of course she will . . . if she loves you," she said wearily. "So devils drive both of us?" She then seemed to cast away all the ghosts of doubt and regret. "I'll be aboard the train when it pulls out," she said briskly. "It would be best if we were not seen together until we reach Marleyville at least."

"How about Leach Valentine?" Bell asked.

"Valentine? What about him?"

"He's waiting below. The ranch surrey is at the hitch rail. I think they expect to drive you out to Spearhead today."

"I'll tell him I have other plans," she said.

He arose to leave, but she halted him. She brought a basin of water and forced him to stand while she did what she could for the new damages he had sustained in his dive from the runaway train. "You might try to keep this cold cloth on that eye," she said, "though I'm afraid it's a little late for that. You're going to have a black optic for your wedding."

Bell thanked her. When he left the room, he found Jenny Walking Elk in the hall, huddled in her shawl. He chucked her under the chin. "Are you one of the devils that drive her?" he asked.

He received only a hostile and suspicious stare.

X

Descending to the street, he saw Leach Valentine look up as he passed the window of the dining room. The blond man's coffee cup paused in mid-rise. Then Bell walked on out of vision. He was wondering at the indifference Nancy Carmody had shown in regard to Valentine. He was also wondering why she had not wanted to go to Owen Randolph for the money. But mainly he was remembering the deep and brooding expression in her eyes when she had agreed that both she and he were driven by devils.

He went to Dan Clark's Boston Store, investigated the clothing rack until he found a dark, conservative suit that fitted him well. "If you can have it ready in an hour, it's a deal," he said.

"Charge it to Mid C."

He added a white shirt and tie, socks, hat, and boots to his purchases. He then moved to a barbershop and was shaved and trimmed. He also rented a bathtub and refreshed himself with a bath. By that time Dan Clark had finished the minor alterations on the new suit and delivered it to him.

When he emerged, his morale had gone up considerably and he knew his appearance had improved enormously, despite the black eye and other bruises.

The first person he encountered on the sidewalk was Alice. She gazed at him, astounded. "Why, Bell, I thought you'd be in Marleyville by this time."

She was on her way to Owen Randolph's office to begin her day's duties and had not heard about the wreck at the Clear Fork. She carried an umbrella to protect her small bonnet that was perched precisely on her neatly arranged hair, for misty rain was falling again. She had on overshoes and held the hem of her skirt carefully clear of the sidewalk. She accusingly eyed his facial damage. Her lips pressed together severely and she tried to move stiffly past him.

Bell blocked her path. "Let's talk," he said.

"It's nine o'clock," she said. "Mister Randolph doesn't like tardiness."

She again tried to move past, but he would not permit it. "So you heard about some of the things that have happened?" he asked.

She did not evade. "Yes, Bell. Mister Randolph stopped by the house last evening and I asked him about the shot we had heard uptown earlier. He said it was fired at you and that you had a street brawl with a cowboy named Shep Murdock."

"You have all the bare facts," Bell said.

"You carry the evidence on your face," she replied.

"If I had let Murdock browbeat me, would you have thought

I had done right?" Bell asked bitterly.

"At least you would not have been in trouble for . . . for . . ." She didn't finish it.

"For once," Bell said.

"Let's not have a scene here," she said. "I must say, Bell, that if it wasn't for the court plaster and the black eye, a person would think you were dressed for a funeral . . . or a wedding."

"A wedding," he said. "Mine."

She moved past him. She had taken this as an attempt at humor that was obscure to her. She proceeded a few steps, then halted as an astounding thought seemed to occur to her. She swung around, giving him a wide-eyed look. Then she hurried onward, and entered Owen Randolph's office.

Bell ate breakfast at the Nugget, then returned to the depot and bought a ticket to Marleyville. He sat on a wooden bench in a corner and discovered that Shep Murdock was in the waiting room, also. The bulky man, whose face bore the marks of their combat, ignored him and stood gazing morosely out at the rain-wet rails.

Bell's seat commanded a view of Main Street. Presently he saw Nancy Carmody emerge from the Mountain House, accompanied by Latigo Jim, who carried a traveling bag. She was followed by Leach Valentine, and he was talking and gesturing vehemently. But she removed his hand from her arm, gathered her skirts, and mounted quickly into the surrey. Latigo Jim tossed in the bag, pulled himself into the driver's seat, and headed the team toward the depot.

Valentine leaped angrily onto his saddle horse and overtook them. Jogging alongside the vehicle, he resumed his objections.

He helped Nancy down at the depot platform and came walking with her into the ticket room. He was red and angry. "Dammit, Nan!" he was saying. "Why go back to Marleyville? You came through there only yesterday."

"I've already told you it was a business matter," she said. "A private matter, Leach."

"It can't be that important. And you can't let me stand around on one foot and then another while . . ."

He now discovered Bell's presence. His voice trailed off as though his mind had swung to some new and demanding thought. Then he gave Nancy all his attention again. "After all," he said, "there's no point in waiting."

"Meaning that I have no other choice except to marry you?" she asked sweetly. She walked to the ticket window. "A round trip to Marleyville please," she said. She opened her purse.

"Quit playing coy and modest!" Valentine raged. "This is no time trying to act like an innocent little girl who . . ."

She turned and slapped him with all her strength. The blow almost staggered him. It left an imprint on his cheek that was dead white.

He said thickly: "Why you . . ." He moved toward her with the fury of a small-minded man. He might have struck her. But he became conscious that Jenks Duvall was staring, pop-eyed, from the ticket booth. He looked at Bell. Then Shep Murdock came in a hurry, grasped his arm, and muttered: "Fer gossakes, Leach."

Valentine swallowed his rage. He pulled a smile from the shreds of his humiliation. "Our first spat, Nan," he said. "I'll have a peace offering waiting when you come home. A ring with a big diamond in it. And a wedding ring, too."

He left the depot then, mounted, and rode up Main Street at a rapid, angry pace. Bell watched him dismount and enter the Crystal Bar. Owen Randolph was striding down the street at his usual erect, vigorous pace, on his way to his office to begin the day. He, too, entered the Crystal for his morning dram of bourbon and bitters. Valentine afterward emerged and mounted. Then he gathered up Shep Murdock's saddle horse from the rack at the Mountain House and rode into a livery.

Bell absently noticed that Murdock himself was no longer in the depot. Then he became absorbed in his own problems.

Nancy moved toward a bench, her course taking her past where he sat. She dropped her kerchief, as an excuse for speaking to him, and, when he arose and handed it to her, she murmured: "He almost struck me, and you just sat there. How ungallant can you be?"

"Considerable, when I'm dressed up in a new suit that isn't even paid for," Bell said.

She gave him a scathing look, and seated herself in a far corner. She wore a wide and dressy hat. Beneath her sealskin coat she had on a very fetching dove gray dress. The wide hat gave her dignity and maturity beyond her years. She sat with gloved hands clasped in her lap. He now saw a loneliness in her.

It was nearly half an hour, despite Jenks Duvall's promises, before the Marleyville train was made ready. A score of outbound passengers were waiting when it finally pulled into the depot. Nancy was the first to mount the steps into the day coach.

Bell chose the smoking section at the rear, which was marked off by a glass partition. Nancy seated herself in the middle of the coach proper. He leaned back as the train got under way. He had missed a night's sleep. Before that there had been many days of hard riding as he gathered his shipment of beef.

He fell asleep quickly. Nancy looked back and her gaze rested on him for a moment. She turned away at once, for she was aware that every move she made would be watched by some masculine eye in the car.

The story of how she had slapped Leach Valentine was now general knowledge, for Jenks Duvall had retailed the account in whispers and with elaborations along with the tickets he had sold to travelers. She was also the person who had displayed her limbs right on Main Street by kicking a steer in the nose. All in all, she had lived up to advance notices. These incidents had only confirmed the gossip that had been flying lately. She was Nancy Carmody, the girl about whom scandalous things were told.

A new rain squall came sweeping down from the benches and drenched the windows. She lowered her head as though dozing, so that the hat brim would shield her. She wept a little. The tears came in a flood. But no one in the car was aware of it.

She finally dried her eyes. She drew from her purse a letter. It had been written some two months previously and had caught up with her just before she had boarded a ship for America at Havre. A cable announcing her grandfather's death had reached her just a few hours earlier.

She read the letter again. It was written in her grandfather's big hand, but the penmanship had been shaky as though the fingers that held the pen had been growing weak and uncertain.

My Darling Granddaughter:

I am writing you now that it is almost too late to ask you to forgive a selfish and intolerant old man for the wrong he did in driving you away from me. I destroyed your mother's happiness and that of my son. I did the same to you by trying to hold you to my own precepts of righteousness and holiness. I was wrong. And I was wrong about your mother. I have heard the calumny that is being whispered about you, and, to my shame, I realized it is my own attitude that gave birth to such evil gossip.

Please come home where we can face these things together. It may be, however, that I have waited too long, and may not be here when you arrive. If so, then Spearhead will be yours. I am making my will tomorrow, leaving everything I possess to you without qualifications. I again ask your forgiveness and acceptance of my bequest.

Your humble grandfather,

Bernard Carmody

She wept again. She knew her grandparent had been aware his days were numbered when he had written those words. She read again the closing message in his letter: . . . LEAVING EVERYTHING I POSSESS TO YOU WITHOUT QUALIFICATIONS. She had gone over that phrase many times since the reading of the will in Owen Randolph's office the previous day. That will was dated only a day later than the date on the letter she held in her hand. She wondered what had happened during those twenty-four hours to induce Buck Carmody to add a qualification to his bequest that was so inconsistent with the tenor of his letter.

The train rumbled across the Clear Fork bridge and she saw construction men standing alongside the track. She realized this was where Bell's cattle had hurtled to destruction. She peered through the window, but all she could see was the slashing rain and the foaming river.

The train climbed Summit grade and topped the crest at a bare crawl. The siding was occupied by the work train and also by a northbound combination train *en route* to Tamarack. This train carried three wooden day coaches instead of the usual single car. Nancy was aroused by shouting and whooping. The men aboard her own car crowded to the windows.

Windows on the side-tracked coaches opened. The majority of the heads that appeared were feminine. These individuals began screaming and laughing and waving kisses. Nancy saw one shapely leg, adorned with striped stockings and a jeweled garter being kicked brazenly in full view.

"Wow!" a man near her was yelling. "Whoopee! Who says the railroad ain't goin' ahead this year? Them's dance-hall gals.

Look! There on them flatcars! More of them ready-built gamblin' houses an' fandango palaces they kin knock down or set up in a hurry at end o' steel."

The painted girls and the men traded jibes as long as they were in sight and sound. Then their train began picking up momentum and the side-tracked coaches fell behind.

Windows closed and grinning men went back to their seats,. talking it over.

"Looks like Mid C might stick to its original route," someone said. "Why else would all them sharpshooters an' gamblers be swarmin' into Tamarack?"

"They got to light some place," another man pointed out. "They kin move fast an' quick anywhere else. I don't reckon Henry Driscoll is tellin' percentage girls an' tinhorns his plans. It's spring, an' they're comin' to Tamarack to be ready to move in any direction the cat jumps."

"I still say it's impossible to build out of the basin north o' town," a man said. "It'd cost 'em a fortune every mile. I say they've got to build by way o' the Clear Fork."

Everyone remembered Nancy's presence then, and fell enviously silent while they contemplated what that would mean to her in the way of increasing the value of her inheritance.

"If I thought Mid C really did aim to stick with the route through Tamarack, I'd be of a mind to cut my gullet with a dull knife," one of the passengers stated. "I bought three lots on the west fringe o' town for two thousand dollars apiece a while back from Owen Randolph. I sold 'em back to him a month ago for a hundred an' fifty, all told. Owen said be didn't want 'em at any price, but hated to see me stuck with 'em for taxes."

"That's about the way it went with everybody," the other man remarked after a thoughtful moment.

After that there was only silence. The lift of spirits had passed.

XI

As the train clattered over the rails, Nancy suddenly became aware that a newcomer had entered the car. It was Clay Irons. He evidently had come aboard at Summit. He looked gaunt and weary. A day's growth of beard added to the austere spareness of his features. He hung his slicker in the vestibule to drip. Returning to the car, he held his chilled hands over the heating stove.

When he discovered her presence, he lifted his rain-sogged hat and said in his soft voice: "A pleasure to see you again, Miss Carmody."

Then he saw Bell asleep in the smoking section and a flicker of surprise crossed his face. He walked down the car, and Nancy watched him stand beside Bell and regard the latter with puzzled concentration.

She surmised that he had some message for Bell, but he decided against awakening him. He folded his lean length into the plush seat opposite Bell, cast his hat on the floor, and gave the car his careful inspection, marking out each man aboard as though cataloguing him. Assured that none of the grudges of the past was riding this train, he huddled in the stiffness of the seat's corner and closed his eyes. Soon he, too, was asleep. Nancy noticed that, even so, his hand rested on one of his holstered guns.

It was mid-afternoon when the train slowed and the conductor announced the Marleyville stop.

Bell aroused and blinked at Irons who had also awakened. "Where did you come aboard?" he asked.

"Summit," Irons said. As was his custom, he asked no questions, but waited for Bell to offer some explanation as to why he was bound for Marleyville and dressed in new garb.

When Bell said nothing, he did not show resentment. It occurred to Bell that Irons was a man who approved of reticence in others.

They descended with other passengers to the station platform at Marleyville. The town was a junction point on the transcontinental railroad and was still booming. Its principal thoroughfare, Lewis Street, had its line-up of saloons and gaudy-faced gambling houses, but in the background two church steeples had made their appearance.

"She's smoothin' down," Irons commented. "I can remember not so far back when Texas cowboys, drivin' longhorns through to the Blackfoot agency in Montana, used to fight railroad men in the streets. It had its man for breakfast quite regular."

The other passengers streamed away, scattering into the town. Nancy Carmody was signaling a horse-drawn cab, and Bell walked to the curb, lifted her traveling bag aboard, and helped her into the vehicle.

"Be in the lobby of the Palace Hotel in an hour," she murmured. "I'll get in touch with you there."

Bell returned to where Irons waited, and they watched the cab move up muddy, crowded Lewis Street.

Irons spoke. "The boys located one cattle car almost intact a couple miles downstream after you left," he said. "There were drowned steers still inside, but what interested us most was that a railroad spike had been shoved into the ratchet of the hand brake so as to jam it." Bell wheeled and looked at him, and Irons added: "I reckon it was the same with the other cars. You told me you had trouble with the brake an' that McGonigle an' Johnson seemed to have hit the same snag. I came to Marleyville to talk to Johnson at the hospital."

He paused a moment, evidently to give Bell a chance to explain his own reason for the trip. But Bell did not speak.

"Word was sent me by the telegraph wire," Irons went on, "that the yardmaster here in Marleyville couldn't find any indication of couplin' failure on the car from which the string broke loose. The cattle cars were equipped with the old link-an'-pin type of couplin' an' so was the car ahead. He thinks the only way it could have happened was that the pin jolted loose. He assumes it was all accidental."

"And what do you assume?" Bell asked.

"I rode up to Summit, after we got horses an' took a look-see," Irons said casually. "Someone left the train there when it stopped after the break. An' someone else was waitin' for him in the brush near Summit with an extra saddle horse. They rode off together. I picked up a few tracks in snowbanks."

"Yeah," Bell said softly. "Go on."

"It had rained hard all night an' blurred the trail so I couldn't do more'n guess what I was seein'. They rode to the wagon road. An' there I lost everything, for half a dozen freight outfits had been over the trail before we reached it an' had cut it to pieces."

"Which way did they seem to be heading?"

"No tellin' for sure. My guess is they were veerin' toward Tamarack. It's only little more'n an hour's ride. A man could have taken two horses out there after dark, picked up his pal who was ridin' the train, an' both could have been back in town without bein' missed."

Bell was remembering his fist fight with Shep Murdock and also his altercation with Sim Gillis.

Irons guessed the trend of his thoughts. "It hardly adds up now, does it?" the Kentuckian said. "It just don't appear like anybody would go that far to get square for what happened in a street fight. Whoever cut that train . . . if it really was cut . . . would know somebody was likely to get killed. McGonigle is dead, an' that makes it murder. You an' Johnson are lucky to be alive. Whatever reason anybody would have for a thing like that it'd have to be big enough to risk the gallows if he was caught.

If you're thinkin' of Sim Gillis, you can write him off the list. I
sent one of the boys into town to check up on him. He was
playin' pool with a couple of railroad men in town last evening."

"Murdock?"

"We couldn't get any exact time on him." Irons shrugged.
"He was in an' out of bars all evening. Nobody could exactly
remember seein' him durin' the early part of the night, but that
don't mean anything."

"What else do you know?" Bell asked.

Irons drew from his pocket a small pillbox, opened it, and
produced two objects wrapped in tissue paper. He unrolled
them, and they lay in his palm—misshapen and metallic.

"Pistol bullets," Irons said. "I dug this one from the plaster in
Miss Carmody's room. It was the one someone fired last night.
The other is the bullet that killed Josh Enright months ago."

Bell stiffened, staring at the battered objects. "Go on!" he
said tensely.

"Pete Jennings loaned it to me last night when I asked him if
he had it," Irons explained. "He believes the case is closed, but,
bein' a dutiful officer, even though he's a little thick above the
ears, he's kept it on file. It was removed from your father's body
at the autopsy." He added in his soft voice: "Both are Thirty-
Eight caliber. Rather a coincidence. Not too many men pack
guns o' that bore. Most of them prefer Forty-Fives."

"Are you trying to say you think that the same person fired
both shots?" Bell demanded.

"Seems mighty far-fetched, doesn't it?" Irons sighed.

"Maybe you're even thinking it might have been the same
person who jammed the brakes on the cattle cars?"

"That seems even more ridiculous when you stand back an'
look at it," Irons admitted. "Likely we'll never know." He
replaced the tissue-wrapped bullets in the small pillbox and
pocketed it. "Anything else I can do for you?"

"I could use a loan of ten dollars," Bell said. "I'm flat."

Irons produced two gold coins. "Twenty would be better, I reckon." Then he drew one of his holstered .45s and placed it in Bell's hand. "I'm a little heavy on hardware right now, anyway," he went on. "Better pack this thing from now on. It's got six live shells in it. Somebody who means business is after you."

Bell looked at the weapon. Then he thrust it in his belt beneath his coat. "Thanks," he said.

He parted with Irons and walked up Lewis Street. Nancy had alighted from the carriage several blocks west and had entered the door of the bank. Bell stopped in an eating house. Well within the hour's time that she had mentioned he strolled into the lobby of the Palace Hotel and took a rawhide-slung chair in the sitting room near a window that looked out on the street.

Neither he nor Irons knew there had been two additional passengers aboard the train. Leach Valentine and Shep Murdock had been riding in the caboose as guests of the conductor who, along with the brakeman, was not averse to accepting a few cigars and a bottle of liquor in return for the hospitality.

Valentine and his companion left the train unseen in the yards, and from the shadow of a freight shed doorway they had watched Bell as he talked to Irons. And they continued to keep track of him as he waited in the hotel lobby.

XII

Through the window Bell had a view of the door of the bank Nancy Carmody had entered for it stood on the opposite side of Lewis Street and diagonally west. An alley bisected the block at this point and both the hotel and the one-story bank flanked this passageway. The clock at the clerk's desk drearily ticked off twenty minutes, then thirty. Bell sat, containing the tension that hummed within him.

Past the window flowed the activity of Marleyville. A brisk wind had blown the rain clouds away. It whipped capriciously at the hats and bonnets of passersby. The first of the month had been pay day at the ranches and also in the railroad shops. The stores were busy. Riders were in town from nearby cattle outfits and cow ponies were tied up in front of every saloon.

Each time the door of the bank opened, Bell's attention quickened. But an hour passed and he was still waiting. Now a raw-boned, long-chinned man came strolling by smoking a cigar and his glance happened to swing to the window. His head came up and he broke stride for a moment as their eyes met. Then Bell pulled his own glance away and the man continued on down the street without looking back.

He was the night turnkey at the county jail with whom the bargain had been made for Matt Barker's escape. This was a chance encounter, for Bell had meant to get in touch with him later. Presently the man, whose name was Sid Durkin, came into the hotel lobby. He carried a newspaper. Seating himself in an adjoining chair, he opened the paper, then spoke in a murmur from back of this shield: "Is the deal on?"

"Yes," Bell said. "I'm waiting for the money now."

"It'll have to be tonight," Durkin warned.

"I'll meet you and Barker at your house at midnight," Bell said. "Bring him there."

"Do I look like a sucker?" Durkin said angrily. "I want to see your money first."

"Where can I talk to you a little later?"

"Make it right after dark at my house," Durkin decided. "I can't risk bein' seen near you again in daylight. I go on duty at the jail at seven." He arose then, murmuring: "I want to see the money then. Don't try to run any sandy on me, Enright. I want cash." He returned to the street and strolled away.

Bell listened to the clock again. Four o'clock came and passed. Across the way the bank had closed its doors to business for the day and drawn its curtains

Bell crushed out his latest cigarette and got to his feet. He decided that Nancy Carmody had obviously changed her mind about the bargain she had made with him.

He found a small, nervous, balding man confronting him. "Mister Enright?" the newcomer asked. "You are Mister Bell Enright, I trust?"

Bell nodded.

"You were described to me, but I was afraid I might be wrong," the man said. "I'm Homer Watts from the Pioneer Bank. Mister Sutton, my employer, sent me to find you. He requests that you come to Judge Burnside's office at the courthouse. Everything is arranged. He said you would understand."

Bell followed Homer Watts to the sidewalk. They walked eastward and encountered Clay Irons. The Kentuckian shook hands with Homer Watts when Bell introduced them, then drew Bell aside.

"I looked at the couplin' where the train broke apart, an' talked to Johnson," he said. "It ended any doubt in my mind. Someone's got it in for you, my friend." He looked at Homer Watts. "Mister Watts, would you an' Enright do me the honor of havin' a drink with me?"

"I'm sorry," Bell said. "I'm meeting some people at the courthouse. It's important and the day is late."

"Courthouse? I hope you aren't arrangin' to sue Mid C for the loss of your cattle. That won't be necessary."

"It's another matter," Bell said. "A wedding."

"Weddin'!" Irons voice lost its softness. He added slowly: "Not you an' Miss Carmody?"

Bell said: "Yes."

Irons's eyes were suddenly bleak. "Of course," he said. "I should have seen it myself. It was plain enough. You in new clothes and the gal all dressed up an' in need of a husband so she could inherit. . . ."

Bell caught him roughly by the arm, halting him. "Don't say any more," he warned harshly, and there was some of the same metallic quality in his dark eyes.

Homer Watts uttered a little frightened squeak and backed hastily away from them, flattening himself against a building wall. Two other men who were passing by stared, then sidled away toward shelter. Clay Irons and his reputation for violence were well known in Marleyville.

He now pushed Bell's hand away. "Congratulations, Enright," he murmured flatly. "You'll be boss of Spearhead. A good marriage for you. A fine match." He turned to walk away. "Did you happen to mention this to Miss Drake?" he added. "Or were you afraid to face her?" Then he moved down the street.

"Come on," Bell said, and Homer Watts, still shaken, fell in step with him.

"I've been told that nobody ever laid hands on Clay Irons without having to pay for it," Watts ventured. "He's a dangerous man. And so polite. Amazing."

Bell did not answer. They picked their way across the makeshift footpath through the mud at the Clark Street crossing and mounted the stone steps of the newly built courthouse. Partly visible at the rear of the county square was the stone-built jail. In this building were the sheriff's offices. And behind the barred windows at the rear Matt Barker waited in his cell.

Homer Watts led the way to the second floor of the courthouse, which was growing deserted at this late hour, and tapped on the door of an office. "This is Judge Burnside's chamber," he explained.

A voice responded, and Watts opened the door and motioned

Bell in. He did not enter himself, but quickly closed the door, and Bell heard him retreating down the hall.

A shaggy-haired, paunchy man with wise eyes sat at a large desk. Also present was another large man in a rumpled and unpressed business suit and a thin, balding man who had a ledger under his arm.

Nancy occupied a chair near the desk. She made the introductions. "Mister Enright, this is Mister Sutton of the Pioneer Bank and Mister Jackson, the county recorder."

The man in the rumpled suit lifted himself up from his chair so that he could face Bell squarely. "I'm Sutton," he said. "I've heard of you, Enright. And of your father."

He gazed at Bell's discolored eye and at the court plaster. His opposition to Bell was very evident. The shaggy-haired man back of the desk spoke. "I am Judge Burnside who sentenced you to prison some two years ago, I believe it was. I imagine you remember me."

"I remember," Bell said stonily.

He looked at Nancy. She sat stiffly in the chair, her hands gripping the arms. Despite her outward composure, he could sense her inner turmoil. She had the heels of her slippers braced against the cross rung of the chair as though to steady them. He was again aware of the tragic loneliness in her—a loneliness and apartness that made her brace herself boldly and challengingly against the world around her.

"Mister Jackson is here to issue the marriage license," she declared. "Judge Burnside will be kind enough to officiate. Mister Sutton and Mister Jackson will act as witnesses."

"Let's get it over with as long as you refuse to heed advice, young lady," the judge snorted. "If Buck Carmody were alive, he'd shoot me for this. Hurry it up, Jackson!"

The formality of the license was quickly taken care of by Jackson. Afterward the judge stood up, Bible open and ready.

"Join hands," he snapped.

He mumbled a jargon in a rapid monotone that Bell barely heard and made no attempt to understand. Nancy's hand in his was cold and lifeless. His responses to the questions were automatic, and so were Nancy's.

". . . by the authority vested in me by this commonwealth I now pronounce you man and wife," the judge concluded, closing the Bible with a snap.

Bell looked into Nancy's gray eyes. There was a sadness and a deep regret in them. Then she lifted her face and stood waiting gravely. He bent down and kissed her. Her lips were taut and without warmth.

He drew back. She tried to smile. "At least that part of it seemed real," she murmured. "Up to now I've wondered if all this was actually happening."

The witnesses silently affixed their signatures. The judge locked his desk and clapped his hat on his head. "Just close the door when you leave," he said glumly. "It's got a night lock."

The three of them tramped off down the stairs, their steps reverberating in the rotunda of the building.

A small leather case stood on the desk. In the deepening shadow of dusk Nancy opened it, drew out several packets of money, and handed them to him. "You'll find the amount correct, I believe," she said. "Twenty-five hundred dollars. It is mainly in ten- and twenty-dollar bills. I assumed you preferred it in small denominations."

Bell accepted the packets and divided them in his pockets. "Why did you assume that?" he asked.

"Money is easier to spend when it comes in small bills," she replied. Her voice was weightless and without inflection. But it represented only a surface calm. Bell knew that she surmised that his urgent need for cash involved something out of the ordinary and that it might be dangerous.

"All this cash and I forgot to pay for the wedding license and to pay the judge for marrying us," Bell said ruefully. "I even borrowed money from Clay Irons just for that purpose."

"No one would expect a flustered bridegroom to think of everything," she said. "However, stop worrying. I paid for the license previously. And Judge Burnside would have refused a fee if you had offered one."

"He has principles, evidently," Bell said. "He didn't approve of me as a bridegroom. Nor did Sutton. How did you browbeat them into coming here?"

"That's another of the advantages that come with being an heiress. People like to do you favors. Particularly bankers. Even judges."

An awkward silence followed. Bell fumbled with his hat. Nancy nervously drew gloves from her handbag and began working them onto her fingers. He knew she was waiting for him to take the initiative.

"Well . . . ," he began, and then lapsed into gloomy silence again.

"We can't just stay here," she said tentatively.

Bell glared at her and felt tiny beads of cold sweat break out on him. She laughed, but it was a forced, artificial gesture.

"Perhaps we should go to the hotel," she suggested.

"Hotel?"

"And take a room," she said. Her voice shook despite her attempt to be crisply matter-of-fact.

"A room?" Bell croaked hollowly.

"A room!" she exploded. "Certainly! We'll have to make a pretense at being married, at least."

"Just pretense, eh?" Bell mumbled.

She burst into a storm of anger. She stamped a foot. "You are deliberately trying to act dense just to embarrass me!

Furthermore, you make me feel like a leper. Am I that repulsive?"

"But Miss Carmody . . ."

That did it. She slapped him as hard as she had slapped Leach Valentine earlier in the day. "The name is Missus Bell Enright!" she panted. "Remember? That's my name as far as the law is concerned. But to fulfill all the legal requirements of marriage we must register at a hotel as man and wife." In spite of herself deep color rose into her cheeks. "I assure you that is as far as it will go," she added.

All the fire and glow of injured pride and infuriated womanhood ran in her. She was breathtakingly alluring.

Suddenly Bell took her in his arms and kissed her, long and hard. This time she was caught unaware. He felt her lips soften and instinctively respond with that promise of completeness that seemed to be always just beneath the surface of her warm gray eyes.

Then she drew away abruptly. "Just what did that mean?" she asked.

"Was that what you wanted?" he said.

She walked to the desk and stood, arranging the contents of her handbag. "No," she said in a low voice. "But . . . does it matter?"

Bell picked up his hat. He offered his arm. "Shall we go, Missus Enright? You are a beautiful bride."

She looked at him, and finally placed a hand lightly on his arm. "Thank you," she said. She added: "We've got exactly what we bargained for, haven't we? You have your twenty-five hundred dollars and . . . and I have Spearhead."

They left the judge's office and walked through the silence of the building to the street. The wind struck them with savage force and Nancy turned against it, grasping her hat with both hands. Bell steadied her until she had regained her balance.

Then they were confronted by the treacherous path of rocks and boards thrown across the muddy width of Clark Street. Nancy paused uncertainly, started to gather her skirts about her, then decided against it. "I'll never make it." She sighed. "There must be better crossings somewhere else."

"That would mean hiking against this wind," Bell said. He bent, lifted her lightly into his arms, and added: "This new suit still isn't paid for. So you can see that I've got to be mighty careful."

He made it safely, although they teetered so narrowly on the brink of disaster in mid-crossing that Nancy uttered a little squeal of dismay.

She was flushed and laughing when he put her on her feet on the wooden sidewalk. "You do like to take chances, don't you?" she said.

"Only on crossing muddy streets," Bell declared.

She gave him a quick, thoughtful look and some of her newly found gaiety faded. She took his arm again, and they proceeded heads down against the cold wind toward the Palace Hotel. They were nearing the hostelry when an angry man blocked their path.

XIII

It was Leach Valentine. His handsome face was livid with outrage. "Just a minute!" he protested thickly. "What in hell are you doing with this fellow, Nancy?"

But he had already guessed the truth. He and Murdock had kept Bell in sight when he went to the courthouse and had waited for him to reappear. Valentine had been curious about Bell's mission there, but had ruled against entering the building because he did not want Bell to be aware of his presence in Marleyville.

The real mission that had brought Nancy to Marleyville on the same train with Bell had never occurred to him. He had seen her go directly to Bill Sutton's bank from the depot and had taken it for granted that she was still there. He had no way of knowing that Bill Sutton had driven her to the courthouse by way of other streets in the banker's phaëton that he kept stabled at the rear of his bank.

But now, seeing Nancy and Bell emerge together, the significance of what had taken place almost beneath his eyes burst upon him. His first reaction was deadly fury. He had been so positive Nancy would fall into his arms when he forced the issue that he had already built his dreams of the future after he and Owen Randolph became the masters of Spearhead. In his deeper reflections he had gone further, visualizing the day when he would be lord of that cattle empire alone, and there would be no Owen Randolph with whom to contend. He now realized that his rage had driven him into a new mistake in revealing himself. But at least Shep Murdock, with no wounded pride at stake, had continued to stay discreetly out of sight.

Bell saw the wildness in Valentine and moved Nancy away from him. "You can be the first to congratulate me, Leach," he said.

Valentine whirled on her. "Don't tell me you're married to him?"

She nodded. "Why, yes. It was just a simple ceremony in Judge Burnside's office a few minutes ago."

"Why, you double-crossing little cheat!"

Bell caught Valentine by the shoulder, whirling him and slapping him across the mouth. That brought blood. Valentine was not only big, but fast and powerful. He kept turning, trying to drive his left elbow into Bell's throat as he spun. Bell blocked that, but Valentine balanced himself and struck for the stomach with a right. Bell could only partly evade the blow. He saw that

Valentine was trying to draw his six-shooter, but was being impeded by the skirts of his coat.

Bell was off balance and also unable to reach the pistol Irons had given him. His only recourse was to grasp Valentine's gun arm. He revolved, carrying the blond man with him along the sidewalk. It was like a crazy dance. Then he released his grip and Valentine went skidding backward on hands and knees off the lip of the plank walk into the mud. Valentine now clawed for his holster and found the handle of his six-shooter.

Nancy screamed: "No! No!"

Bell steadied himself and flipped open his coat. His hand was on his own pistol. "Go ahead, Leach," he said.

Valentine remained motionless. He saw that he held no advantage and that, if he went ahead with his draw, both he and Bell were likely to die. He decided to wait for a better time. He let his hand move carefully clear of the weapon and got to his feet. "I'll make your wedding night one you'll always remember, Enright," he said. "I'm going to beat you to jelly with my fists. Shed your pistol. It'll only slow you down."

Valentine started to unbuckle his holster. But Clay Irons came running to the scene, accompanied by a graying, heavy-shouldered man who had a badge pinned to his vest. This was Jim Hennessy, sheriff of Minaret County.

"Break it up, you two buckos!" Hennessy was shouting. Then he added: "Oh, it's you, Leach." His tone became respectful, as befitting a public official addressing the foreman of the biggest taxpaying ranch in his jurisdiction. Hennessy identified Bell and frowned. "Trouble seems to hound you, Enright, don't it? Or maybe you just hunt for it. A night in the cooler will settle you down."

"If there's any charge against my husband," Nancy spoke, "I'll go bail for any amount."

"Husband?" Jim Hennessy was shocked. "Ain't you Miss

Nancy Carmody?"

"Until very recently," she said. "I'm now Missus Bell Enright." She looked at Valentine. "You're discharged, Leach. I'll name a new foreman when I get back to Spearhead." She smiled engagingly at the sheriff. "I hope you've changed your mind about arresting my husband," she said. "After all, it was self-defense. This fight was forced on him." She linked her arm in Bell's. "In fact, I'm rather sorry you interfered," she said. "Mister Valentine's manner was very annoying." She looked up at Bell. "Come, darling. After all, this is our wedding day. Let's not have it spoiled."

Irons had said nothing. He watched Nancy and Bell walk away, a look of wariness and speculation in his eyes.

Bell and Nancy proceeded to the hotel, finally stopping at the clerk's desk. "A room, please," Bell said, his voice shaky. Nancy nudged him, and he hoarsely added: "The bridal suite, if you please."

The clerk, a long-necked, freckled young man, stared, then said hastily: "Of course. And congratulations, Mister . . . Mister . . . ?"

His voice faded off into thin silence as he read the signature Bell had just penned on the register.

"Mister and Missus Bell Enright," Bell said.

The confused clerk led them upstairs to a sitting room and sleeping room much like the one Nancy had occupied at the Mountain House in Tamarack. The front windows overlooked Lewis Street and the single window to the left opened upon the darkness of the alleyway.

"We'd like supper served to us here," Bell told the clerk.

When they were alone, Bell touched a match to the shaded lamp on the stand. Its subdued light eased the stiffness of the furnishings.

Nancy removed her hat and fluffed out her hair. "I'm happy

you ordered the supper here," she said tiredly. "I couldn't have faced the stares in the dining room."

Bell stood near a window, gazing down on the street. The sidewalks were almost deserted. The cold wind and the approach of darkness had driven the people of Marleyville indoors. The cow ponies at the racks stood forlornly, tails to the wind.

"Why was Valentine in Marleyville today?" he finally inquired.

"I imagine I was the reason," she said reluctantly. "He was curious about my business here, no doubt."

"Was he on the train with us?"

"I didn't see him," she said. "He may have been in the caboose with the train crew. He probably didn't want me to know he was keeping an eye on me. He . . . he was sure I would marry him."

"And why didn't you?" he asked.

She moved to a mirror, drew out objects from her handbag, and began doing things to her eyelashes and lips. "Why should I have married him?" she asked at last.

"He's smart, not bad-looking, and he knows cattle," Bell said. "Even people who don't cotton to him say he's a good man on the range."

"Is that what you say about him?"

"What difference does it make what I say?"

"Perhaps a woman looks for a little more in a man than whether he can rough a herd of cattle through a hard winter or nurse a sick steer through a siege of colic," she said.

A waitress came to the door. "Steak, boiled chicken, fried ham, venison, elk stew, or trout?" she said. "An' plum pie. I put up the plums myself last fall. Wild ones."

"A menu to be remembered on your wedding night," Bell said. "No fuss or feathers. Just solid grub."

They named their preferences. "And a cake," Bell added. "If there's one to be had in town. One with white icing preferred."

"Cake?" the woman said blankly. "A piece of cake?"

"A whole cake," Bell said. "A wedding cake!"

He maneuvered her out of the door then, and closed it. Nancy busied herself at the mirror again. "That wasn't necessary," she finally said. "The cake, I mean."

"On the contrary, the occasion calls for special ceremony," he said. "It isn't every day that we get married. You paid for the license and used your influence to force a judge into performing the ceremony. I notice that you even bought a wedding ring somewhere. At least the supper should be on me."

"The ring is the one my mother wore when she married my father," she said slowly.

Bell winced. He stood gazing at the gold band on her finger. "I should have known," he said. "My father once told me that your mother was one of the prettiest girls he had ever seen."

She gave him a look that was almost tragic. "Perhaps we'd better talk about the . . . the weather," she said. "It might be safer . . . and less upsetting."

She went into the bedroom and closed the door. Bell heard her stretch out on the bed to rest. He rolled cigarettes and watched darkness come over the town.

The waitress brought the meal and carried in a small table upon which to serve it. They ate in silence. "We seem to have exhausted all subjects of common interest," she commented.

Full darkness had come. Bell pushed back his chair. "Will you excuse me?" he asked. "I have a business matter that I must take care of."

"But your wedding cake?" she protested. "It hasn't arrived!"

Suddenly he realized that the cake had become important to her. "I know," he said. "I'm sorry."

She arose, smiling in that brittle way that he was beginning to realize was only a shield for a hurt. "I take it that this is the finish of our brief honeymoon," she said.

Bell nodded. A constraint now held them and her face was carefully empty of all expression. This was a parting, an ending. He was remembering that moment when he had carried her across the muddy street in his arms. He recalled the cold neutrality of her lips when he had kissed her at the conclusion of the marriage ceremony, and that moment later on as emotion had swept over them when he had kissed her again. He was deadened by a knowledge of aimlessness and futility. He held out his hand. "Good luck," he said.

Her gray eyes inspected him, troubled. "That sounded as though we might never see each other again," she said.

"That would solve one problem for you, at least," he said.

"Problem?"

"Of ending this marriage gracefully. You could claim desertion."

"Or perhaps I could also be a widow," she said.

Bell said nothing.

"That's the way it might be, isn't it?" she said. She slowly placed her hand in his. "You are the one who will need this good luck that you mentioned. Does this thing you intend to do have to be done?"

"I don't know what you're talking about," he said roughly.

"I've seen this trouble in you ever since we first talked yesterday," she said. "Whatever you intend to do is outside the law. You had to have cash in a hurry . . . but not for yourself."

He moved to the door.

She held him a moment longer. "If anything happens, I'll tell Alice Drake that . . . that this was not a real marriage," she said. "That it meant nothing to you . . . not the way a marriage is supposed to mean."

That broke through Bell's armor. He looked at her and said: "Everybody has lied about you, haven't they? And I've been wrong about you."

Again he kissed her. Slowly this time—and gently. Then he turned and went out and closed the door between them.

XIV

Bell believed he was unnoticed as he left the hotel. He headed westward up Lewis Street through the windy darkness, disciplining himself to move without undue haste, although he was feverish with impatience. The packets of money were bulky in his pockets. He thought of that other coat, similarly laden, which lay at the bottom of the Clear Fork. He would soon know whether all he had gone through had been worthwhile. Or whether it had been worth nothing.

After three blocks he turned off Lewis Street into a cross street, and moved south along this thoroughfare into an area given over to rather shabby habitations and vacant lots. The moon emerged from the clouds and cold, bright light glinted on the roofs, forming square shadows in his path.

He knew the way to Sid Durkin's house, for it was at a whispered parley in the man's kitchen nearly two weeks in the past that he had heard the terms for clearing the way for Matt Barker's escape. The sidewalks were mainly of cinder, with occasional stretches of planks to bridge the muddier spots. The neighborhood was still busy with its supper chores and there were window lights to mark out some of these hazards.

A barking dog suddenly exploded in a fenced yard at his elbow. His gun was in his hand and he was ready to shoot before his mind could identify the sound. He thrust the weapon back in his belt, and moved along. The dog returned to its kennel and peace came again.

Presently he flattened against the splintery face of a board fence. He fancied he had heard the *crunch* of footsteps behind him. He could see nothing. Presently a door opened in a house in the middle distance, letting a streak of lamplight slant into the street. A man's silhouette entered and a woman's querulous voice said: "It's about time. Supper's waitin'." The door closed. Another door opened, and he heard the *splash* of dishwater being thrown into a yard. Somewhere a baby was crying.

Presently he came to a small gabled house. It was built of planks and bats and in need of paint and stood a dozen feet off the sidewalk, guarded by a fence of sagging chicken wire. A plank walk led to the doorstep and another such path angled around the corner of the house toward the rear.

He surveyed the area to make sure he was unseen, then made his way around the house. There a lean-to kitchen overlooked a barren yard. The outline of a wagon shed loomed at the rear.

He tapped on the kitchen door. It opened quickly and Sid Durkin said: "Come in! I was beginnin' to fear you'd yellowed out."

The kitchen was small and smelled of grease. An oil lamp stood on a table among soiled dishes. Durkin bolted the door and motioned Bell to a chair at the table. "Ain't nobody else here," he murmured. "I sent the old woman to visit her sister on the other side o' town."

Bell preferred to stand. "I've got the money," he said. Bell stacked the packets of bills on the table. "Count it," he said. "But it stays there, and I stay with it until Barker is out of jail and I talk to him."

Durkin counted the money and his grin turned greedy. "I'll fetch Barker," he said. "It might take time before I figger it's safe. You kin wait here."

"How are you going to explain his escape?" Bell demanded.

"I ain't in this alone," Durkin said. "The deputy on duty in the office tonight, Art Whalen, is cuttin' in on the money. Barker will have a six-shooter. We'll slip it into his cell. He's to git the drop on me an' force me to unlock the cell. That's for the benefit o' the other prisoners in nearby cells. He's to march me into the office, where he's supposed to leave me an' Whalen tied an' gagged while he makes his gitaway. But I'll fetch him here, an' then go back to the jail where me an' Whalen will tie each other up an' wait for someone to find us."

"This gun that Barker's to get . . . ?" Bell began.

"It won't be loaded," Durkin said. "Don't you think we got any brains? If Matt Barker ever got his paws on a loaded hog-leg, you'd never see him ag'in. He ain't a bit interested in whether me an' Whalen ever collect that twenty-five hundred dollars. An' I don't reckon he's anxious to talk to you, either, if he can git out of it." He eyed Bell shrewdly. "An' I been wonderin' just why it's worth so much money fer you to talk to him," he added.

"Keep wondering," Bell said.

"Whatever Barker knows must be mighty hot to be worth that kind of dough," Durkin said. "Say, it wouldn't have anythin' to do with the killin' of Josh Enright last fall, now would it?"

Bell looked at his watch. "You mentioned that you were to go on duty at seven. It's nearing that now."

Durkin arose, showing his teeth again in a knowing smirk. "Fact is, Matt sorta said as much to me not long ago when I was talkin' to him. He was braggin' that he knew who shot your father."

"I'll be waiting here," Bell said. "And this gun of mine is loaded. You can believe that."

Durkin's grin was unchanged. He drew on his coat, and said: "Better blow out the lamp. Then it'll look like nobody's at home in case some neighbor gits a notion to come callin'."

Bell extinguished the lamp and, after Durkin had left, settled down in the gloom of the frowsy kitchen.

Once again time dragged. He found there was no pleasure in smoking in darkness. He thought of Nancy Carmody, remembering her as she had stood looking at him, her eyes concerned for him. Again he found his mind dwelling on the moment when he had carried her in his arms, close against him, her figure firm yet soft and very desirable. Then Alice's blue eyes, frank and honest, came out of this medley of thoughts, gazing at him questioningly and hurt. That brought him back to reality. The strain returned, bearing harshly down upon him. He became conscious again of the slow grinding pace of time and the discomfort of the stiff chair and the musty, unclean odor of this house.

He added more wood to the greasy cook stove. The red glow that flickered from its apertures dimly lighted the room. An hour passed. Then two. He knew the neighborhood was turning in for the night. The wind had died. Occasionally the dog in its enclosure down the street broke into its aimless yammering. The wailing of the baby had ceased long ago. From the far direction of Lewis Street came the slap of spurred hoofs and the whoop of some celebrating cowboy.

Another hour passed slowly by. Then he heard them coming. It was the faintest scuff of movement on the foot walk outside the house. A hand tapped softly on the door and Durkin's voice murmured: "All right!"

Bell opened the door. His pistol was in his hand. An overcast was moving across the sky, dimming the moonlight, but his eyes, tuned to the gloom of the kitchen, recognized the bulky, bull-necked man who stood with Durkin. It was Matt Barker.

Barker spoke in a hoarse mutter: "You waited till the last minute to show, didn't you, Enright?"

"I had my troubles," Bell said. Within him now was a singing excitement. For even in the few words Barker had uttered was a sureness. The man apparently had no qualms about his ability to go through with his part of the bargain. He knew the identity of the men who had murdered Josh Enright and was prepared to reveal it.

"Git inside before someone sees us," Durkin was muttering impatiently.

He started to guide Barker into the door ahead of him. And then it happened.

Guns opened up from the shadow of the wagon shed, their roar breaking with the violence of an unexpected thunderclap. An invisible force lifted Matt Barker and shoved him roughly ahead through the doorway into the kitchen. He uttered an agonized, gasping grunt. His weight fell against Bell. Supporting the man with his left arm, Bell drew the six-shooter Irons had loaned him, and fired twice into the yellow-hot gun flashes that continued to flicker from the corner of the wagon shed.

He could feel Barker's body quiver and vibrate as though a harsh and ponderous hand was slapping him on the back. Each succeeding convulsive trembling was another bullet hammering out the man's life.

Bell twisted around, pushing Barker aside from the open door, out of the line of fire. He remained there himself a moment and fired a third shot. The ambushers' guns continued to blaze blindingly. Bell heard bullets smash objects in the kitchen back of him and knew these must have missed him by scant inches.

Sid Durkin was reeling, clutching vainly at the frame of the door for support. Slowly he sank to his knees. From that position he managed to draw his pistol. He emptied it in a wild, booming volley, but the bullets went into the sky for they had been fired only by the reflex action of a man in the last quivering instant of his life. Then Durkin pitched forward into the doorway on his face.

Bell grasped him by the shoulder, intending to drag him to safety inside the kitchen. Then he felt the hard rake of a bullet as it tugged at his skin like a burning brand. He fired twice more above Durkin's body at the flickering gun flashes coming from the shed. Then something as solid as a thrown paving brick struck him in the left side. The breath was driven out of his body and he collapsed backward in a ludicrous, staggering fall.

The shooting ended abruptly and the silence that followed was as incredible as had been the sustained roar of the guns. Bell crawled to the door and tried to close it, but Durkin's soggy body blocked the threshold and now he did not have the strength to move it. He knew Durkin was dead.

Barker gasped in that bubbling manner: ". . . someone set a . . . a deadfall. . . ."

Bell moved to his side and said: "Barker, this is Bell Enright. Can you talk?"

A vengeful anger kept Matt Barker alive a second or two longer. "Enright," he breathed. "Enright, it . . . it was . . . it was . . ."

And that was all. Barker had tried to reveal the name of Josh Enright's killer and had failed. Now Barker was dead along with Durkin.

Bell gradually became aware that his own wound was deep and harsh. Blood was soaking his shirt. He knew what it would mean if he was found here with an escaped prisoner and a jailer lying slain on the floor.

He backed through the house and opened the front door. The dark street was still deserted, for the echoes of the gunfire had scarcely ceased reverberating over the town. No nearby neighbor had as yet dared show his face.

He ran across the muddy street and halted, crouching in shadow, and watched the Durkin house. The sticky flow of blood was increasing and he began to fight nausea. He had hoped to see the men who had hurled that fusillade of death into the kitchen door. But nothing moved around the house. The assassins evidently had retreated westward through the shabby fringe of the town.

At last he heard men approaching from Lewis Street. He moved away, entering a vacant lot between houses, seeking a path to streets to the east.

Behind him an authoritative man boomed: "Where was that shootin'?"

"At Sid Durkin's house!" someone yelled quaveringly.

Bell was beginning to stagger now as dizziness assailed him. A window curtain parted and a glare of lamplight caught him vividly in its flood. The heads of a man and his wife appeared there. They were so near he could see their startled expressions. He broke into a run. The woman screamed. He crossed another street, then a vacant lot. He kept stumbling ahead.

He finally halted, fighting the weakness that was pervading him. After a time he saw a flicker of lanterns and bull's-eyes in the distance. The couple who had seen a bloody man run past their window had given the alarm.

The hunt for him had started. He again heard the strident voice shouting: "Take no chances! He's already killed two men an' one of them was an officer of the law. Shoot on sight an' shoot to kill!"

That was Jim Hennessy, the sheriff. Bell forced himself into motion again. The excitement and the cry of the search kept building up. And the shock of his wound was heavier on him now. He found himself colliding dizzily with fences and houses.

The numbers of searchers was increasing steadily as more men kept pouring into the side streets. Many of the cowboys had raced from the bars to join in the chase for the sake of excitement, for he could hear their shouts and the spatter of hoofs in the streets around him.

One of them rode by, shouting: "It was a jail bust out! Sid

Durkin shot it out with a feller named Matt Barker an' a pal. Durkin was murdered an' Barker is dead, too. The killer got away, but he was hit."

Bell's objective was the railroad yards on the east side of town. However, the search had spread in that direction and its growing pressure drove him northward along a dark and muddy alley. Presently he realized that this lane opened on Lewis Street where gambling houses and saloons still blazed with light just ahead.

The Palace Hotel stood at the near corner and he crouched against its wall, his knees shaking, trying to subdue the harsh, gasping effort of his breathing.

He crept to the corner of the building and risked a look into the street. The sidewalk was empty in the immediate vicinity. Not all of the cowpunchers were mounted and hunting him. Three cow ponies were only a dozen feet from where he crouched, standing hipshot at the rail in front of the hotel.

Bell tried to summon his flagging energies. He meant to make a run for it, leap into the saddle, and ride for open country. Instead, he reeled and sagged against the wall. There was a roaring in his ears; with an acid feeling of regret he realized that he had gone over the edge. In another few minutes the man-hunters would find him here.

Then a figure darted into the lane from the lighted street and came rushing directly toward him. He tried to lift his six-shooter. "Don't come near me," he mumbled.

"It's me," a small and frantic voice breathed. "It's Nancy Carmody." She pushed the gun aside and knelt beside him. "You're hurt! You're covered with blood. I . . . I heard the shooting and guessed you were in it. I watched from the windows and saw you here. Something told me when you left that . . . that . . ." She didn't finish it. "I'll get a doctor," she said.

Bell caught her arm, held it desperately. "Did anyone see you come down here?" he gasped.

"I don't think so," she said. "Everybody rushed out of the place when the shooting began. Even the clerk. My window is right above and . . ."

Bell saw that she was hatless and had not even stopped to pick up a jacket. "Go back," he said thickly. "Get away from me. Don't get mixed up in this." He tried to get to his feet—and failed. His thoughts were growing wild and irrational. "The men are dead," he mumbled. "Two of 'em. They'll hang me for it. They're coming. With lanterns and guns."

"Hang you?" she said in a high tone of horror. He nodded mutely, still fighting for breath. She gripped his arm, bending her head close to him. "There are horses in the street. Can you ride?"

Bell tried to laugh at that. He tried to think of something devastatingly humorous to reply. But all he could say was: "I can ride anything that won't throw me."

She left him. Dully he watched her move to the corner and peer out. Then she walked casually onto the open sidewalk and out of sight.

After a minute or two she returned, leading a pair of the cow horses he had seen at the rail. No shout of discovery arose.

That inspired him. He pulled himself to his feet.

"Here," she said in a taut whisper. She guided his foot into a stirrup. It was mainly her lithe efforts that got him onto the horse. He desperately grasped the horn and she hung onto his belt, keeping him propped in the saddle until his head quit spinning.

He straightened. Now that he had the great strength of a horse under him, he felt the shadow of those prison bars recede. "I'll dance at your next wedding," he mumbled.

He struck the horse with the ends of the reins and it leaped into full stride, carrying him into Lewis Street. He found that she was stirrup to stirrup with him. She had mounted astride in her skirts and the skirts were fluttering and her hair was flying loosely. Even in that moment of stress it brought back his memories of the wild-riding young girl who had passed him so many times in the past without ever giving any indication that she had noticed him.

In a croaking voice, that he tried futilely to form into a shout, he again ordered her away from him. But all she said breathlessly was: "Hurry! Hurry!"

XV

They made it across Lewis Street and into the mouth of the opposite alley. Then someone shouted an alarm. But they were racing at full gallop northward through the dark lane between buildings. The echo of their passage came hurtling back into their ears from the enclosing walls.

Far behind them now the person who had discovered their flight came cautiously to the alley and fired two random shots down its dark length. Then the enclosing fences and buildings faded around them and they were rushing through a nondescript area of scattered hovels and open fields.

But the shots that had been fired brought the manhunters pouring from the south side of town into Lewis Street. The man who had sighted the fleeing figures was a case keeper at a faro bank in the Palace Hotel's gambling room.

"It was two of 'em," the man kept repeating. "One was wearin' somethin' that was flyin' almost like a loose slicker." Sheriff Jim Hennessy arrived. Two cowboys now discovered that their horses were missing.

"That proves there really were two of 'em anyway," the sheriff said. He looked around. "I'll have to swear in about a dozen of you riders," he said.

He began pointing out men. Leach Valentine appeared in the crowd. "Count me in, Jim," he said. "And I'll donate my dollar a day back to the county."

Clay Irons had joined the bystanders, also. Jim Hennessy looked at him. "How about you, Clay?"

Irons shook his head. "No," he said.

Irons walked away and entered the Palace Hotel. Everyone was on the sidewalk, watching the activity in the street where Jim Hennessy was organizing the pursuit. He paused at the desk, swung the register around, and found the room number the clerk had penned on the line where the names MR. AND MRS. BELL ENRIGHT had been signed.

He climbed the stairs and made his way to the door of that room. It stood partly ajar. He tapped, and, when there was no answer, he stepped inside and closed it behind him. A lamp burned on the stand. On a small table stood a cake with white frosting that bore candles. They had never been lighted. Irons gazed at this for seconds with his pale gray stare.

The bedroom door stood open. A lace nightgown was laid out on the bed. A silver-backed brush and a matching comb and other items were on the dresser. Nancy's handbag was open. Her sealskin jacket hung in a closet and her handbag lay on a stand, along with the key to the room. Irons appropriated the key. He paused to gaze again at the wedding cake, and there was a wondering question in him now. Then he went out, closed and locked the door, and dropped the key in his pocket.

He returned to the street. Presently he watched the man-hunters gallop out of town. The cowboys were still enjoying this.

Bell was forced to cling to the saddle horn as they raced onward. Nancy rode at his side, a hand gripping his arm to support him.

"Can . . . can you hang on just a little longer?" she almost sobbed.

Bell showed her a death's-head grin. "I'll hang and rattle."

They passed the last scattered buildings and the horses were running freely across an open flat. The lights of Marleyville burned brightly behind them. Overhead the clouds were luminescent with the glow of the moon.

Now Nancy veered eastward and led the way across a ridge. Presently the shadow of a solid line of brush appeared ahead, marking a stream.

She called a halt at last, alongside a creek that rushed by coldly in the night. "Now," she said.

Bell tried to slide lightly from the saddle. Instead, he pitched head foremost. A boot hung in a stirrup and the horse started to spook, but Nancy freed his leg in time and quieted the animal.

She knelt beside him, found his book of matches in his shirt pocket, and struck a light. "Oh . . . oh," she moaned. The match was snuffed out by a stir of breeze. She looked up at the overcast sky and said fervently: "Please! Please! I've got to have light. He's dying!"

But there was only the faint and eerie luminescence. She removed Bell's coat, tore his shirt away, and explored the wound with her fingertips. By sense of touch she found that the bullet had torn a long and deep gash along a rib. It was still bleeding and she could feel the hard presence of the slug beneath the flesh at the back. The wound on his arm was only a scratch.

She removed her petticoat, ripped it into strips, and used them to bandage the wound and check the flow of blood. She paused, listening to the distant sound of horses being ridden at a long lope out from town. This sound strengthened and bore nearer, becoming a scattered danger as men circled.

Finally the clamor veered northward and she returned to her task. She believed Bell was still unconscious, but he spoke now in the strained labor of a man who had to frame each word. "You can't do this. You can't stay with me. They'd never forgive you."

"Lie still," she said. "You'll start the bleeding again." She gazed up at the overcast in mute but fervent appeal.

Presently the moon rode through a rift in the clouds and gave her fifteen minutes of brilliant light. That permitted her to bandage the injury more effectively.

It was an ugly wound, and had damaged two ribs. He had now lapsed into a semi-stupor from shock and loss of blood. She brought water in her cupped hands from the creek and moistened his lips. He aroused and slowly returned to full awareness. He saw that she was shaking in the increasing chill of the night, for she was wearing only the handsome gray dress—her wedding dress.

"This is as far as you can go," he said thickly. "Head back to Marleyville before you're missed. Two men were shot down back there. I didn't do it, but that won't matter."

"Who killed them?" Nancy asked.

"I'm not sure. I didn't see them. But there were at least two of them. They were shooting to burn down all three of us. I was the only one who came out of it alive." Haltingly Bell told her the full story of Matt Barker. "You've got the right to know the truth," he said. He sat looking at her, but his thoughts were on that moment when the guns blazed. "Why were they staked out there?" he muttered.

He pulled himself to his feet. He reeled, then steadied. The effects of shock were passing, now, leaving only the weakness and the hot and tearing pain. But he could think clearly.

"Where are we?" he asked.

"About three miles north of town. Mounted men came searching just west of us a while ago, but finally headed on north up the trail."

"They likely don't count on having any luck until daylight," Bell said.

"Which means that we've got to find some good place to hide before the sun catches us," she said. "We've got a few hours."

"It means that *I've* got to find such a place," Bell said. From the distance the wind brought the mournful wail of a locomotive whistle in the Marleyville yards. He aroused. "That's one way a man can outrun a horse," he said.

"They'll probably be watching the trains," she objected.

"They can't watch every mouse hole on such short notice," he pointed out. "And I've got to take my chances no matter which way I go."

He moved to a horse, got his foot in a stirrup. After two attempts he gave it up. But Nancy came to his help and boosted him into the saddle.

"I'm out of condition," he gasped. "Not getting enough exercise lately."

"You've got to get to a doctor," she said. She sounded as if she was sobbing.

He glared at her threateningly, for she was mounting the other horse again. "Good bye," he said. "And thanks for everything. I can never pay you back, of course."

"That's hardly the way to treat your wife on her wedding night," she said.

"That's paid for and finished. Remember?"

"Follow me," she said. "I'm familiar with Marleyville and its geography. I was even born here . . . in what is referred to in polite circles as a house of ill fame. My grandfather refused to permit the child of a dance-hall singer to be born in the hallowed confines of Spearhead. My father brought my mother to Marleyville by stagecoach. It was a small cattle town then, and there was no other place my father could find to shelter her

127

when the baby started to arrive. My mother died that same night. But the girls in the place pulled me through. It was not until after my father had died of grief that Grandfather took me in." She touched her horse and moved ahead. "Yes," she added bitterly, "I know Marleyville very well. And Tamarack and their people. They've branded me as a wanton woman."

"That's past," he said. "You're the owner of Spearhead now. They'll kowtow to you. You're risking too much."

"I'm risking nothing," she said. "They never condemn a woman for standing by her husband. I may even be credited with being self-sacrificing and noble. That might offset some of the other things they say about me." She twisted in the saddle and gave him a faint smile. "After all, we *are* man and wife in the eyes of the world, you know."

Bell forced his horse into the lead. The stream ran, wide and shallow, over gravel and they rode through water to leave no trail. They headed down the creek. Clouds obscured the moon again, but after a time he made out the spidery outline of a railroad trestle ahead. This was the Mid C's route northward toward the end of steel at Tamarack.

They now swung toward town, leaving the creek behind, and keeping the track to their left. Presently the railroad yards opened before them, with switch lamps gleaming, red and green and yellow, in the night. A westbound train was pulling out on the main line.

"If I could have boarded that one," Bell said, "I'd have been in Oregon . . . or maybe California in a few days."

"You'll be dead before another day unless we find a doctor," Nancy said. "That bullet must be removed . . . and soon."

"I'll promise you one thing," Bell said. "I'll never die until I learn why Matt Barker was burned down tonight before he had a chance to tell me who killed Josh Enright."

"Look," Nancy breathed. "Isn't that a train on the Tamarack

line there at that water tank?"

They rode closer. "It is," Bell said. "Freight train, northbound. Sent by heaven."

He slid from his horse and again found himself fighting against waves of weakness. He held her stirrup to assist her in dismounting. But he was too optimistic. His head began spinning again, and it was she who was forced to descend in a hurry and grasp him to prevent him from falling. He clung to her desperately until the world quit revolving.

"If we weren't married, I might be forced to slap you for trying to become too familiar," she said.

"You can't go on with this," he croaked.

"I might say that your devotion leaves something to be desired," she said. "You seem to do nothing but try to get rid of me."

"Any man who gets you for a real wife can thank his lucky stars," he said. "But I won't stand for letting you . . ."

She exclaimed: "Hurry! It's pulling out!"

Lanterns were swinging. Metal *clanged* as the hatch on the tender's water tank *banged* shut. The engineer fed steam to the boilers and the locomotive lurched ahead, rocking the first section of cars into motion.

Bell broke into a run, stumbling across lines of sidetracks. His feet were as heavy as logs. Nancy ran at his side.

The entire string was heaving into motion as they reached the shadow of the train. Flat cars came lurching slowly past, riding heavily beneath loads of steel rails. Then gondolas appeared, carrying new cross-ties piled high and braced with cables. Bell realized this train was moving the railroad's own supplies to the end of steel at Tamarack. It was further proof that construction was to be resumed.

Boxcars swayed into view and some were empty with doors partly open. "Our only chance," Nancy breathed.

She scrambled agilely into the black maw of one of the moving cars, then caught his wrists and helped him drag himself aboard. He flopped on his face on the floor of the dark car, his lungs sobbing for air while she sprawled wearily beside him.

After a few minutes he summoned the strength to crawl to the open door and peer out. Marleyville's lights were falling astern.

"Let's hope they don't come across those two horses until morning," he said haltingly. "It looks like nobody sighted us when we got aboard."

But someone had seen them. Back in the Marleyville railroad yards a thin, lone man stood in the darkness alongside a shanty. It was Clay Irons. He watched the receding lights of the train dwindle northward.

He had realized that Sheriff Hennessy had left one sizeable loophole in the cordon of posse men that had been sent out to ring the town. He had gone to the railroad yards himself and had arrived in time to watch from a distance as two dim figures boarded the departing train.

He had made no move to halt their flight. He began absently tossing in his hand the key with which he had locked the bridal suite at the Palace Hotel while he stood considering his course. Searching around in the weedy area beyond the last line of railroad sidings, he located the two cowponies Bell and Nancy had left ground-tied.

Gathering up their reins, he led the animals along back streets to the west end of town. Awaiting his chance, he tied them at the rail of a saloon on the far fringe of the business district two blocks from the Palace Hotel where they had been originally left by their riders.

XVI

Bell sat, leaning against the wall of the swaying car. The train was hitting a steady pace now and the roar of the wheels was a hollow thunder in the dark space around them.

Nancy lighted one of his matches. In its glare she peered closely at him. She found a scrap of loose packing paper on the floor of the car. She twisted this into a spill, lighted it, and in that lingering illumination examined the bandages she had contrived. She said nothing but he saw a deep dread in her face.

He realized that she was shaking uncontrollably in the cold. "You're freezing," he said in a gust of self-accusation. "And I never gave it a thought."

He painfully pulled off his coat and, although she tried to refuse, insisted on wrapping it around her.

"That's the first time you've ever been warmed by twenty-five hundred dollars," he said. "It's all there, still intact. And it's all yours. I didn't need it after all. The man I was going to give it to never lived to get his hands on it."

Nancy closed the sliding door but the chill wind found its way to them nevertheless. Slowly he felt the cold creep into him. She huddled against him for warmth, and he wrapped his arms around her and drew her closer.

That helped. He finally fell asleep in that position. It was a stupor rather than sleep. At times he mumbled thick and wild words. "Look out! Look out! They're killing us! Barker, look out!"

Nancy spoke soothingly. "You're safe now. And alive."

Bell murmured longingly: "Alice! You're so lovely! Don't ever go away again."

Presently his sleep became quieter, more restful. But Nancy remained awake, gazing unseeingly into the darkness. The car rumbled on through the night carrying them farther away from the manhunters at Marleyville—carrying them back to Tamarack.

It was an hour before daybreak when the train entered the Tamarack yards. Bell aroused. He still held Nancy in his arms. She had only recently fallen asleep. Her head lay against his chest and she gripped one of his arms with both of her hands.

She now awakened, also. She looked up at him, and at first a wondering smile formed. Then memory came back with all its harshness and she drew abruptly away from him.

He revived his numbed muscles, and at last was able to move to the door and peer out. The train was slowing to a crawl.

"Time to be leaving," he said. His voice sounded far away, although he tried to be brisk. The roaring had started in his ears again.

They dropped to the ground together and he sprawled woodenly, unable to summon the power to get to his feet. She lifted him with a strength born of desperation, pulled his arm over her shoulders, and in that manner supported his staggering weight. They reached the shadow of a string of cars on a siding and huddled there for a moment to make sure they had not been seen.

"Just a few minutes longer," Nancy was saying. "Then we'll have help for you."

"Where . . . ?" he mumbled.

She did not answer. He knew they had left the railroad yards and were moving through the back streets of a town. All thoughts were wild and aimless now and it was his belief they were still in Marleyville with Hennessy and his posse at their heels.

A small voice kept sobbing and praying. With a shock he realized that it was Nancy. Conscience-stricken, he tried to pull away from her, tried to tell her that he could make out now. But she kept her hold on him.

Then they were standing before a door and she was tapping cautiously. It was a kitchen door. His dull mind decided they were back at Sid Durkin's house. He remembered those blazing guns and he waited for them to open up again.

Instead, he heard a girl's voice, sharp with apprehension, respond inside the house. "Who is it?"

Nancy answered in a fierce whisper. "It's Nancy Carmody. And . . . and Bell Enright. He needs help."

That pierced the fog in his mind. This was not Sid Durkin's house! That was 100 miles away. They were standing at the rear door of Alice Drake's home in Tamarack!

Horrified, he tried to turn away. But Nancy refused to release him. "There's no other place," she breathed. "If she loves you, then you should trust her that much. You're bleeding again, and I can't stop it without help."

The door opened. Alice stood there, a lamp in her hand, a dressing robe pulled over her nightdress.

Nancy forcibly drew Bell into the kitchen. She closed the door and said: "Make sure all the curtains are drawn, Alice. No one must know we came here."

Alice looked at the crimson bandage and at Bell's gray features. All color had rushed from her own face, but there was no screaming and no revulsion in her. "You're hurt, Bell!" she said in horror.

Alice's mother appeared. Teresa Drake was a small, pert woman, with bright eyes and a very active mind. She, too, wore a dressing gown and her graying hair hung in braids. As the wife of a two-fisted man engaged in the rough-and-tumble profession of wagon freighting she was no stranger to violence and blood and injury. In addition to that, she had been a girlhood friend of Bell's mother and that friendship had continued even after the marriage to the dashing outlaw, Josh Enright. Teresa Drake was one of the few who had openly declared that Bell had been unjustly sent to prison.

She turned him now so that she could inspect him in the lamplight. She flew into action. "We'll put him in your room, Alice!" she exclaimed. "Get the bed ready. Hurry. He needs help . . . and fast. He's been shot."

"Shot!" Alice exclaimed

"We'll need a doctor," Mrs. Drake said. She looked at Nancy. "You're dressed . . . though I must say you seem to have been through something mightily strenuous yourself, Miss Carmody. Your pretty dress is ruined, and that's a shame. Go fetch Ulysses Sylvester at once. Roust him out of bed and tell him Teresa Drake said she'll cut off his ears unless he hustles. You know where he lives, don't you? He's still in the same house as when you were a young girl in this country."

"I remember," Nancy said.

"No doctor," Bell mumbled. "No doctor!"

"Where is your father, Alice?" Nancy asked.

"Away on a freighting trip to Round Valley," Alice said. She had moved to Bell's side and was brushing back his matted hair. "He'll be gone several more days."

"I'll bring the doctor," Nancy said. "The bullet is still in him. It's been hours since he was hurt. He's been through so terribly much since."

Bell tried to bar the way to the door. "I can't have anyone come here," he said hoarsely. "Not even a doctor."

"Ulysses Sylvester won't talk," Nancy said. "He's an old family friend. And he also will respect the power of wealth. You've got to have expert attention."

Then she was gone. Bell found that now it was Alice who was steadying him. "What happened, Bell?" she asked. "Who shot you?"

"Never mind that now, dear," her mother said, taking Bell's other arm. "Let's walk him upstairs. I'll undress him while you get water heating and bandages ready."

"Why is Nancy Carmody with you?" Alice insisted.

Bell started to say that Nancy Carmody meant nothing to him or he to her. But he realized that this was no longer true—at least as far as he was concerned. Not after what they had gone through together.

"We were married yesterday in Marleyville," he said.

"Married? You? Nancy Carmody?" Alice's voice rose to almost a scream.

"It was a cash deal," he said, and now each word was a great effort. "It was . . ."

The roaring began in his head again and now it caught him up in its violence and smothered him. All events became disconnected.

At long last he realized he was lying on white sheets in a dainty bedroom, and the heavy seamed face of the old cow country doctor, Ulysses Sylvester, was floating above him. He remembered pain—driving, excruciating pain.

He heard the doctor say: "There it is. A Forty-Five slug, or I never saw one. And I reckon I've taken a hundred or more of 'em out of men."

He saw Alice's eyes, their blueness darkened with apprehension, looking down at him. Then Nancy's face, wan with strain, came into his line of vision.

This aroused him, and, after trying several times, he forced himself to talk. "I'll tough it through," he told Nancy. "I wouldn't want to let you down after you packed me all that distance trying to save my worthless life."

Those were his memories. He recalled watching Ulysses Sylvester straighten with a tired sigh and say: "He'll make it. He'll likely strengthen fast after you get some broth and then some beef in him. And all the canned tomatoes, strained, that he wants. It was mainly loss of blood that got him. Another hour and it would have been too late. His kind come back fast from a thing like this. He'll be on his feet in a day or two."

That was his last recollection, for he drifted away and knew nothing more for many hours.

After the doctor had left, Alice and Nancy sat facing each other across the table in the kitchen. They had coffee cups before them. Teresa Drake had removed the breakfast plates and the food that none of them had more than tasted, and then had gone to her room knowing they wanted to talk alone.

Nancy broke the stiff constraint. "Bell Enright and I went through a marriage ceremony in Marleyville yesterday," she said. "We registered at the Palace Hotel to complete the legal requirements. That was all. We parted then. Our marriage was nothing more than a strict formality to meet the provisions of my grandfather's will."

"He said something about it being a cash deal," Alice said. "Now I understand. Or do I?"

Nancy winced a trifle, but went ahead. "The idea was entirely mine," she admitted.

"Why him?" Alice asked curiously. "I was not aware you two were even acquainted."

"Apparently he needed money urgently," Nancy said. "Necessity forced him to accept my offer."

"Why are you telling all this to me?" Alice wondered.

"Last night, when he was half delirious with pain, he spoke your name. He said . . . 'Alice, you're so lovely!' "

Alice's eyes suddenly misted. It was a little while before she dared speak again. "Thank you for telling me that," she said. "But I understood you to say that you and he parted after this . . . this technical marriage."

Nancy's lips were stiff and straight, but she refused to let any emotion come into her voice. "Some hours afterward I found him wounded in Marleyville," she said. "I believe that is all you should know right now."

"You don't trust me, do you, Nancy? Or do you prefer being referred to now as Missus Enright?"

"I prefer to be called Nancy Carmody," Nancy said slowly. "In my own heart I am still unmarried. As for trusting you . . . ." She appraised Alice for a time with her cool gray gaze. "I don't know you very well, Alice," she finally said. "Even though we are the same age and were born and raised in this country and saw each other often, we never really became acquainted. You always were looked upon as a good girl . . . a model of virtue. And I was a wild one. How I used to envy you."

"Envy me?" Alice cried incredulously. "You, the granddaughter of Buck Carmody? Why, in mercy's name?"

Nancy shrugged. "As a child I used to watch the way the boys looked at you . . . respectfully. The way Bell Enright looks at you. But boys never looked at me that way. You were the kind of girl they pictured in their minds when they thought of growing up and marrying. I'm the kind they thought of in other ways."

Alice was sitting up straight, her lips very tight, her blue eyes flashing.

Nancy went on: "No, Alice, I don't know you well enough to trust you. A person like Doctor Sylvester won't talk because he is not only an old friend, but he respects the punishing power of wealth. And anyone who inherits a ranch like Spearhead is supposed to be wealthy. But, to you, wealth means nothing compared to virtue. I feel that, if you decide that a man should be turned over to the law, then you would do it . . . no matter how near and dear he might have been to you."

Alice was crimson, shaking. "I'm a prim little namby-pamby," she said. "That's what you're trying to say, isn't it? I'm damnably respectable! I'm frigid. I'm sickeningly virtuous and shallow. So upright that I'd turn my own lover over to the law to spare my own name from any stain. I'm not a flesh and blood woman . . . like you are a woman. That's what you believe, isn't it?"

"Until proven otherwise . . . yes," Nancy replied icily.

They stood measuring each other.

"At least you are frank," Alice said. "Are you in love with him?"

"I told you that it was your name that he mentioned when his need was the greatest," Nancy said. "I'm sure that must mean a great deal to you."

"In other words, you would not admit it even if you were in love with him," Alice said. "Apparently you must have risked your life to help him."

"I am legally his wife," Nancy said. "For the sake of appearances I could do nothing else."

"It never seemed to me that you ever cared what other people thought about anything you might do," Alice said.

"You could be wrong there, also," Nancy warned.

Again they stood estimating each other.

"And you could be just as wrong about me," Alice declared firmly. She glanced at the clock on the wall. "I must be getting to the office!" she exclaimed. "It's nearly nine o'clock. I don't want to be late today of all days. I'm not good at thinking up excuses. Mother will find some of my clothes for you. We're about the same size. And . . ." She broke off, for consternation had appeared in Nancy's expression.

"Good grief!" Nancy moaned. "I forgot. My own clothes are still in a room at the Palace Hotel in Marleyville! We could, perhaps, have explained anything else but that. They'll find them sooner or later." She realized she was saying too much and quit talking. Alice uttered an impatient and protesting sigh. Then she left the house.

Mrs. Drake presently brought a tin bathtub into the kitchen

and poured warm water into it. "It'll settle you down, you poor dear," she told Nancy. "You're still all a-tremble. An' no wonder, from what you must have gone through by the looks of both of you when you got here."

Afterward she wrapped Nancy in a warm flannel nightgown and put her to bed in her own room across the small hall from where Bell was resting.

Nancy lay, thinking despairingly of the personal effects she had left in the hotel at Marleyville. Even her handbag was still there. And, above all, the wedding license. Eventually the room would be opened. Then Sheriff Hennessy, if he did not already suspect, would know the identity of the wounded man and the companion who had eluded his posse.

Finally exhaustion claimed her and she slept. Across the hall Bell muttered in his pain-racked stupor. "Nancy! Nancy!"

XVII

Dusk of that same day found Owen Randolph still seated at his desk in his secluded small, inner office. The main office was closed to business for the day, and Alice had gone home.

Owen's hands stretched out before him, opening and closing as though he longed to have a throat in his grasp. He had been drinking—an unprecedented amount—but his mind was crystal clear. His fury was greater than any such stimulation. His features, in this moment, were no longer fine-cut. Black temper drove a hard and discoloring blood into his temples, staining his skin, changing its texture to a meaty, raw hue. Brutality glittered in his narrowed eyes.

Across the table Leach Valentine and Shep Murdock sat in the stiff, straight chairs that Owen preferred for his visitors. They had returned from Marleyville by train earlier in the afternoon and had entered Owen's office by the rear door. Their expressions were taut and distinctly uneasy. They watched Owen's anger, awaiting its unpredictable climax. Murdock had not been in a position to visit a barbershop, for he had remained out of sight in Marleyville, not caring to advertise his presence there. He had stolen a ride in an empty boxcar on the return trip to Tamarack, while Valentine had paid his fare and taken a seat in the coach.

Valentine still wore his mud-spattered boots and saddle garb in which he had ridden with Jim Hennessy's posse on the futile search for Bell. There was no fear of Owen in his demeanor or in Murdock's. Or deference. Valentine had eased his chair around and let his right hand rest on the rim of the desk, a position from which he could drop his palm to his holstered pistol with a minimum of wasted time. Murdock, also, was ready for anything. Neither of them wished nor expected it would come to that. But they knew the deadly capabilities of the man with whom they were allied. A faint, wicked smile framed Valentine's lips as he listened.

"I should have known you'd mess it up, Leach," Owen concluded. And he brought both palms slapping hard and angrily down on the desk.

"And, of course, you could have done better, Owen?" Valentine queried with edged politeness.

"I counted on you to at least make good on the easiest part of it," Owen said, his voice thick with his choking rage. "I set it up for you, arranged for you to feather your nest for life. You not only let Enright slip out of your hands, but you let that girl walk off and marry him. You, with your boasting about your way with women! Bah!"

"We're even on that score at least, Owen," Valentine said.

"Even? What do you mean?"

Valentine's derisive smile deepened. "I saw you leaving the Mountain House the other evening like a whipped pup after you had talked to Nancy Carmody. I know now you had told the truth when you said you hadn't shot at Bell Enright that night. But you fired the gun, nevertheless."

"So you're keeping track of me as well as Enright."

"You tried to double-cross me by asking her to marry you, didn't you, Owen?" Valentine went on. "If she had accepted you, then you'd have tried to shut us out in the cold."

"Hardly," Owen said coldly. "I fear we three can never be rid of one another that easily. One of the penalties we must pay is that we stick together no matter how repugnant it might be to our personal feelings. The reason I asked Nancy to marry me was that I had begun to doubt your ability to win her over. And my fears were obviously justified. However, I was not surprised by my own failure. After all, she's a mere child, comparatively."

"Child?" Valentine laughed jeeringly. "Owen, as much as you love money, you'd give everything you own if she'd have you." He added bitterly: "And so would I." His gaze met Owen's defiantly. "Shooting at that window was a mistake," he said. "You were the child at that moment, Owen. You let that devil's temper of yours get out of hand at the wrong time. Do you want to put all our necks inside a rope?"

"Is this a diplomatic way of telling me you intend to do the thinking from now on and give the orders?" Owen inquired scornfully.

"Maybe," Valentine said. "We can't afford any more blunders, either yours or mine. Bell Enright came mighty close to taking both Shep and me out of circulation in Marleyville. He had nothing but the flashes of our guns to aim at. We hadn't figured he'd be able to lash back at all, let alone that fast. One slug glanced from the barrel of Shep's six-shooter as he was holding it. Another tore into a post right alongside my face. A fraction, either way, and he'd have punched both our tickets. We should never have let him stay around this long."

Shep Murdock nodded. "He's a sight more swift with a gun that I figgered," he said in his surly voice. "Must 'a' learned it from his paw. Josh Enright wasn't a man you took any chances with."

"Nor Clay Irons, either," Valentine said grimly.

Owen straightened. "Irons?"

"He was in Marleyville yesterday." Valentine nodded. "Snooping around. He was on the train with me when we came back to Tamarack this afternoon."

Owen sat, frowning. The choleric hue in his cheeks faded. He began thinking again, coldly, precisely. "There's nothing to be gained by squabbling among ourselves," he said. "Let's end the recriminations and quit crying over spilled milk. We're had a setback in our plans in regard to Nancy Carmody and Spearhead. I am not, by any means, giving that up as a lost cause. There may be ways by which this so-called marriage can be attacked. But that will have to wait. This other matter cannot."

Valentine nodded. "Mid C is getting ready to move. The town's full of gamblers and boomers. The railroad is assembling a construction gang at Marleyville, boarding them in bunk cars. Some people here in Tamarack are beginning to wonder already if they weren't too hasty in selling property back to you for a song."

"The secret can't be kept forever," Owen said. "Henry Driscoll will make the formal announcement any day. We can't risk any further delay."

His tone was brisk, cheerful. But Valentine and Murdock sat, heavy and brooding, in their chairs.

"Let's go over what took place in Marleyville last night," Owen said, keeping his voice carefully low. "You're certain that Matt Barker didn't talk to Bell before . . . before the event?"

"We've gone over it a couple of times already," Valentine snapped irritably. "We started shooting after Enright opened the door. We threw plenty of lead to make sure Barker didn't have any chance to talk. Durkin stopped some of it, and so did Enright. But Barker got the most of it. He likely never knew what hit him."

"I hope you're right," Owen said grimly. "But, after all, Enright was in that doorway, too, and he left there alive."

"But hard hit," Valentine pointed out. "And he knows nothing to talk about even if he's able to talk. Maybe he's dead of his wounds in some hole he crawled into."

"Do you really think he's dead?" Owen asked hopefully.

"No," Valentine said. "Not yet at least. I think Nancy is with him somewhere."

"What?" Owen, startled, come halfway to his feet. "That seems incredible. What makes you say that?"

"I told you about that case keeper who said he saw two people riding fast down an alley," Valentine said. "He claimed one of them seemed to be wearing a loose slicker. I think he was really seeing a girl's skirts flying as she and Enright fogged it out of town."

"Where . . . how . . . ?"

"I don't know where he found her or how she found him," Valentine admitted. "I only know she was missing from the Palace Hotel all night. At least, if she was in her room, she wouldn't answer the door. I went up there before I started out with Hennessy's posse and again when I got back in town long after midnight. Nobody would answer my knock. The door was locked."

"But those two cow ponies?" Owen argued. "According to the story that came over the railroad wire from Marleyville today the belief that two persons had escaped on stolen horses failed to hold up. The two 'punchers were mistaken about their mounts being missing. They had only left their horses at another saloon."

"I don't figure they were mistaken," Valentine said. "I took a look at those two horses myself this morning. I found a few specks of dried blood on one horse. And some more on the saddle horn. Also, a couple of threads were snagged in a buckle on the latigo of the saddle on the other horse. Gray threads. Nancy had been wearing a gray dress."

"You mean they circled back and left those horses as a blind."

"Could be. Or maybe someone did it for them as a favor."

"Who?"

"I don't know. I wish I did."

"Why, it's plain enough where they're hiding!" Owen exclaimed. "She has him in that room at the Palace in Marleyville. They probably were in there all the time when you knocked."

"I thought of that, too," Valentine said impatiently. "I went back to the room this morning to make sure. But I found the door wide open and a chambermaid working inside. She said that Nancy and Enright must have checked out early. I talked to the clerk, and he hadn't seen them leave, either. But they had left the key on the desk along with money in an envelope to pay for the lodging."

"But if Enright was wounded, he couldn't have walked out with her without attracting some kind of attention, no matter what hour they left," Owen protested.

"They were never in that room, at least after Enright was hit," Valentine said. "The chambermaid said it had not been slept in by anyone."

There was a silence. "Where do you think they are?" Owen asked.

"A Mid C train carrying construction material pulled out of Marleyville last night about ten thirty," Valentine replied. "I learned that later. It was one loophole Jim Hennessy overlooked. That train reached Tamarack before daybreak this morning."

Owen came completely to his feet. "You think they're here . . . in town?"

"Maybe. Maybe he's been here and is gone. If he's alive, he's got to hole up somewhere until that bullet wound heals. That's the only real evidence to connect him with the affair in Marleyville. Eventually he'll head for the one place he figures nobody. knows about. Then we'll have him."

Owen relaxed a little. "Of course," he said. "But we must find him as soon as possible."

Shep Murdock spoke uneasily. "What difference does it make about Enright now? Barker's dead. Nobody but the three of us knows anything."

"Enright only needs to know one more fact, and then he will know everything," Owen said quietly. Then he added: "And Irons, also."

"Irons?" Valentine repeated wryly.

"You said he was snooping. I fear he may have learned enough already to begin adding two and two together. Like Enright, he lacks a reason for events that have taken place. I am sure Henry Driscoll has not taken even Irons into his confidence in the matter which Murdock here said was known only to the three of us. But it will all be plain enough to Irons as well as Enright eventually." He paused, then added curtly: "If they are still alive."

Again there was a long silence. "You pick it tough," Murdock finally muttered. "Enright. An' now Irons."

"None of us can be connected with this matter," Owen said. He looked at Murdock. "You once mentioned a person named Blackie Fergus who might be employed for certain purposes. Is he still available?"

"He's still in town." Murdock nodded.

"Can he be depended on? And at what price?"

"Maybe two hundred. He'd enjoy the job. Irons slapped him

around at Julesburg a couple years back."

"A hundred should be sufficient." Owen sniffed.

Thus was a death sentence pronounced not only on Bell Enright, but also upon Clay Irons.

XVIII

Bell slept until late afternoon, arousing when he heard Alice return from her day's duties at Owen Randolph's office. Nancy arose from the bed in the room across the hall and came tiptoeing to gaze in at him.

He stared at her blankly, then summoned a blurred attempt at a grin. "So that's the way they dress in heaven?" he croaked. "Maybe I'm not going to like it here, after all. Where are the wings?"

"You're being sacrilegious as well as rude," Nancy said. "Missus Drake loaned me this nightgown. It was very decent of her."

Bell eyed the garment. It was made of cotton and quite voluminous. It hung in folds and covered Nancy amply from chin to ankles.

"Decent is the word," he agreed. "That wasn't the kind I saw in your traveling bag at the Palace Hotel on your wedding night."

"Now you're being vulgar." Nancy sniffed. "And it is apparent that you are much improved in health, now that you are taking so great an interest in such things as nightgowns. You know where you are, of course?"

Bell nodded. "I know," he said. "And it's the last place in the world I'd have picked. What day is this?"

"We came here this morning before daybreak. The doctor removed the bullet."

"Doctor? I remember now. It was Ulysses Sylvester. What did you tell him?"

"I said I shot you accidentally during a lover's quarrel."

"And he believed it?"

"Of course not. But he won't talk."

"What about Alice and her mother?" he demanded. "Did you tell them also it was a lover's quarrel?"

"They didn't ask. Teresa Drake is just a jewel. She only sniffed when I tried to apologize for imposing on them. Do you know, I believe she actually likes you."

Alice and her mother had heard the murmur of their voices and now came up the stairs. "You look better, Bell!" Alice exclaimed happily. "Very much better."

"I could stand some more improvement," he said. "I feel like I didn't duck fast enough when the stampede came my way."

"I'll just bet you're wolf hungry," Teresa Drake said. "I'll fetch some broth. I really think you'll appreciate it."

"That will do for a starter," he said enthusiastically. "Then ham and eggs, if it isn't too much trouble."

"That will come later," Teresa Drake said, beaming. "Broth now. You'll be well in a hurry. When you start thinking of your stomach, there's not much to worry about."

Nancy left the room. Afterward, dressed in one of Alice's frocks, she went to the kitchen. Alice was there alone, preparing supper. Twilight had come and every curtain in the house was drawn tight.

"Bell's sleeping again," Alice murmured. "Mother has gone to the store." Presently she spoke again. "There was quite a lot of excitement in Marleyville last night. The news came over the railroad telegraph wire today."

"News?" Nancy asked innocently.

"There was a terrible gunfight. Two men were killed. One was named Sid Durkin, a deputy who worked as a turnkey at the county jail. Someone had smuggled a gun to a prisoner named Barker. He forced Durkin to release him from his cell and tie up the other deputy who was on duty in the jail office.

For some unknown reason they went to Durkin's home. Evidently Barker had an accomplice waiting there and a battle started. Durkin must have managed to grab a six-shooter. They found his body and that of Barker there at Durkin's house. But the other man escaped."

Nancy displayed no outward expression. "I'll make coffee," she said. "Where do you keep the grinder?"

"On the shelf just over your head," Alice said. "The accomplice was wounded. They found traces of blood. At first, it was believed he and still another person had escaped on stolen cow ponies. A man even claimed to have fired two shots at them as they rode away. Posses hunted them the biggest part of the night and are still casting around Marleyville, but now they think the wounded man never left Marleyville at all."

"Why do they think that?" Nancy said.

"The two cowboys who thought their horses had been stolen later found them tied up at another saloon a couple of blocks away. Jim Hennessy cussed them out for being drunk and forgetful."

"Tied up at another saloon!" Nancy exclaimed. "But . . ." She halted. "Very interesting," she finished lamely, and began revolving the handle on the grinder. The aroma of freshly prepared coffee mingled with the other homely fragrances of a meal nearing completion.

"They say that whoever freed Barker and killed the turnkey will surely hang if he's caught," Alice said. Her voice was drawing out thin now.

When Nancy made no comment, Alice resumed talking. "There was another piece of news from Marleyville today. It caused an even bigger sensation in Tamarack. It was the announcement of your marriage to Bell yesterday. Also that the bridegroom and Leach Valentine had engaged in a jealous fist fight in public right after the ceremony."

Again Nancy made no comment.

"I never saw Owen Randolph as upset as when he heard about your marriage," Alice went on. "He walked into his office and slammed the door hard enough to break the glass. Evidently he disapproves of your choice of a husband."

"Evidently," Nancy said.

"You know when to hold your tongue," Alice remarked. "They say such wives are worth their weight in gold."

"I'm worth more than that if what they say is true about the railroad being forced to build west up the Clear Fork," Nancy said wearily. "And all it cost me was twenty-five hundred dollars to buy a temporary husband."

"The money is still in the coat you had around you when you came here with Bell," Alice said slowly. "It seems that he never got to use it for whatever he needed it."

"Apparently not," Nancy said.

"There is also a six-shooter in the coat," Alice said. "With only one live shell in the chamber. It could not have been fired more than four or five times. I'm no expert, but I've done some target shooting and some hunting with Dad, and know a little about guns, having been taught to clean them and take care of them."

"What do you mean?" Nancy asked slowly.

"Matt Barker and Sid Durkin were hit by many bullets, according to the story," Alice said.

"The person who killed them could have used more than one pistol," Nancy pointed out.

"Yes," Alice said. "He could. But that remains to be proved."

Nancy suddenly moved to her and kissed her on the check.

Alice was amazed. "Now, why did you do that?" she asked.

"I'm beginning to understand that respect in Bell's eyes when he looks at you," Nancy said.

"Respect be damned!" All of Alice's prim reserve had

vanished. Her eyes were bright and color burned in her face. "You really thought I'd give him up to the law, didn't you? That's what a straight-laced prude such as you think I am would do, isn't it? I must be above reproach at all costs. You say you envied me when we were children. Did it ever occur to you that I also envied you? Not only as a child, but all my life. Even now! At this very moment!"

"What are you saying, Alice?"

"And did it ever occur to you," Alice went on fiercely, "that I wanted to be looked at as they look at you . . . as a women of flesh and blood, a woman to be desired, not venerated! A woman they can laugh with and love and kiss, who will give them loyalty and affection and all the things a man really wants in a marriage. Respect! Heaven save me! That's the burden a cold and unwanted woman bears."

Alice's mother returned at this moment. She saw their expressions and wisely said nothing. The three of them soon had the supper on the table. They ate in silence, fearing that even the most casual topic might lead them into deep water.

Full darkness came. In the room above, Bell aroused again and lay listening to the scrape of dishes as the evening chores were taken care of. Pain was still with him, but now it was an annoyance rather than a burden. He was very hungry. Alice came to peer in at him presently and he said: "I'd give a red pony for a thick steak."

She placed her hand on his forehead. "Your fever is down," she said. "In fact, it's about gone. Ulysses Sylvester said you'd wake up with a fierce appetite. But before you start thinking of your stomach, you ought to thank your lucky star that you're still alive."

"I thank my lucky star for sparing me, and also for the steak I hope to get," Bell said.

Alice laughed. She brushed his cheek with her lips. "Do you

think I'm nauseatingly respectable?" she asked.

He scowled at her. "Something tells me that no matter which way I answer that I'm going to be knocked kicking," he said. "That question is loaded on both ends."

"Do you?" she demanded determinedly, hands on hips.

"Nauseating is a term that could never be used in connection with you in any sense of the word," Bell said. "Here's the other cheek to kiss."

"You have won that and also the steak with that flattering way of side-stepping," Alice said.

Afterward, he was eating the steak with relish, propped upon pillows in the bed, when Ulysses Sylvester tapped discreetly on the kitchen door and was admitted.

The doctor came upstairs and examined him. "Another stretch of sleep will do you more good than all the doctors in creation," the medical man stated. "I'm not needed here as long as you take it easy and let that injury heal normally."

Ulysses Sylvester departed, plainly glad to shed the responsibility of this patient. Bell finished the meal and rolled a smoke while he tried to piece together the hectic sequence of events.

Then he heard a new visitor come to the parlor door and twist the handle of the bell. Nancy retreated up the stairs. She came into the room and stood alongside the bed. Both of them listened to the voices below.

Teresa Drake had gone to the door. "Why . . . why . . . it's Mister Irons!" she exclaimed, confused.

Irons soft voice said: " 'Evenin', Missus Drake! 'Evenin', Alice!"

There was a brief moment of awkward silence. "Come in, Clay!" Alice exclaimed heartily. "What's that you're carrying? Why, it's a pack sack."

"Brand new," Irons said. "I bought it in Marleyville. I'm wonderin' if you'd oblige by permittin' me to leave it here with you folks for a spell?"

"Here? Why, of course."

"Just until you see Miss Nancy Carmody," Irons said.

"Nancy Carmody?" Alice's voice faltered a trifle.

"I should have referred to her as Missus Bell Enright. You've heard of the weddin', of course?"

"I heard," Alice said.

"I've got some articles in the pack sack that belong to her," Irons said. "A woman's travelin' bag an' even her handbag and such-like. There's a pretty nightgown. I piled the whole caboodle in the sack in order to avoid answering silly questions an' brought it from Marleyville."

"From . . . from Marleyville?" Alice stammered.

"I thought you might be the first to see them when they got back from their honeymoon," Irons said.

Bell lifted the six-shooter from the pocket of his coat that hung beside him on a chair.

Nancy breathed: "Oh, no." Then she descended the stairs and walked into the parlor. "You were right, Mister Irons," Bell heard her say. "I am here already."

Bell strained his ears, waiting, the pistol still in his hand.

"I hope you'll find nothing missing, Missus Enright," Irons said blandly.

"I'm sure everything is intact," she said. "How did you come by my belongings?"

"Part of the railroad's service," Irons said. "You overlooked some of your luggage when you checked out of the Palace Hotel. You must have left early. The clerk appreciated your courtesy in leavin' the money for the room on the desk."

"It was clever of you to guess where to find me," she said. "Newlyweds pride themselves on outwitting their friends during their honeymoon."

"I'm afraid anybody who really hankers to find you will figure it out sooner or later," Irons said. "If you want peace an' quiet, it might be well not to stay here too long."

"Perhaps you're right," Nancy said shakily. "Thank you."

"I hope nobody's ailin' seriously," Irons went on. "Is it your husband, Missus Drake?"

"My . . . my husband?" Alice's mother stammered. "Why . . . why do you say that?"

"I saw Ulysses Sylvester's old top buggy tied up a ways down the street a while ago, an' fancied I saw him comin' out of your front gate," Irons said. He flashed a somber smile. "Well, I must be going. Good night, ladies."

"Wait until I get a wrap," Alice said. "I'll walk with you to the gate."

"There's a moon, almost full," Irons said, and, although his manner was light, there was a sudden wild hope in his voice. "An' you're a right pretty girl. No tellin' what might come of gate swingin' on a night like this."

Alice tried to laugh lightly, but in her again was the awareness of the emotions that ran beneath the surface of this tall, remote man who was called a killer by some people.

Bell heard them move across the porch. The parlor door closed. Nancy came up the stairs with a rush. She was pale, quivering with excitement.

He had slid the pistol out of sight. "Now what did all that mean?" he muttered.

"He knows you're here, of course," she breathed. "It was a warning that you won't be safe here very long and also that visits by Ulysses Sylvester might be a giveaway."

"He seems to know I was mixed up in that shooting in Marleyville," he said. "How?"

"He knows and he seems to think someone else knows, also . . . and is still after you."

"Then why doesn't he turn me in?" he muttered. "After all,

153

he's a sort of law officer himself."

"He helped cover up for you instead. He must have removed my belongings from that hotel room and left the money to pay the bill to make it appear that we had spent the night there and left early. He also must have been the one who found those loose cow ponies and tied them up in town to confuse Jim Hennessy."

She had told him earlier about the mysterious reappearance of the horses they had ridden out of Marleyville. It had been one of the items in the puzzle that he had not been able to fit in. But now it meshed with Irons's action in regard to Nancy's luggage.

"He said anybody who really wanted to find me would figure out sooner or later that I was here in this house," he said. "How?"

"*Cherchez la femme*," Nancy said casually. "Look for the woman. Irons is aware of your affection for Alice. He decided you would naturally turn to her for help."

"Is that why you brought me here?" he demanded. "Because there was nobody else I could trust?"

"Yes," she said unshrinkingly.

"Bring me my clothes," he commanded. "I'm leaving here."

"Because of Irons's warning?"

"Because it isn't fair to Alice to stay. They might come after me at any moment."

"Who are they?"

"The law for one. A jail turnkey was killed in that fight in Marleyville. That will be laid at my door. And there might be others after me."

"There *are* others, and you know it, and so does Irons," she said fiercely. "Who are they? Why are they out to kill you?"

"I wish I knew for sure," he said. "I . . ."

A six-shooter slammed heavily in the street, the flash winking against the window curtain. Alice screamed wildly outside the house.

Bell scrambled from the bed, snuffed out the lamp, and parted the curtain to peer out the window, all in one motion. The pistol exploded twice more. The flashes came from a low stone wall that protected a neighbor's yard across the street.

Bell heard the slugs smash into the clapboards of the Drake house below. Alice screamed again. Now he saw her, crouching behind the inadequate protection of the picket fence in the Drake yard. Irons was on one knee above her, holding her down with one arm so that she could not rise and further endanger herself.

Then Irons left her and leaped the fence and raced across the street in a reckless rush upon the position of the bushwhacker.

The assassin fired two more frantic shots, but Irons kept running and weaving. He was an elusive shape in the moonlight, darting as relentlessly upon his quarry as the swoop of a falcon.

At the last moment, the other man reared from cover and tried to flee. This was the issue Irons had forced. The man fired his last shot, and Irons also fired a single bullet. The ambusher missed even at that close range, but Irons's bullet found its target. Bell saw the figure across the way go pitching headlong to the ground.

Irons vaulted the stone wall, then pulled up and stood gazing down at something at his feet. Bell moved back from the window and drew Nancy with him deeper into the darkened room. Presently men began to gather around the spot where Irons stood.

Bell heard Alice enter the house. "I'm not hurt, Mother," she said, "but someone tried to kill Clay."

XIX

Presently Pete Jennings arrived and began giving orders in his heavy voice. After a time a body was carried away and the onlookers began to drift away, still talking about it.

Bell heard Jennings and Irons enter the parlor of the Drake house. "I'm mighty happy you wasn't hurt, Miss Drake," Jennings said.

"Only my dignity," Alice said. "Clay pushed my face right into the ground. I hardly even know what happened."

"Clay says he had trouble with this fella a couple of years ago back at Julesburg," Jennings said. "It looks like he tried to pay Clay off. Men who enforce law an' order have to expect things like that once in a while."

"Then he's dead?" Alice's voice was wan.

It was Irons who answered: "Yes."

"He should have knowed better'n to miss with his first one when he threw down on Clay," Jennings said with a grisly attempt at lightness. "After that it was like tryin' to hold off lightnin' with a broomstick. Say, you look kind o' peaked, Miss Drake . . . hey! Grab her! She's faintin'!"

There was a stir and a tramping of feet in the parlor and excited voices.

"All right," Irons said. "I've got her. I'll lay her on the sofa."

"I'm . . . I'm all right now," Alice said feebly. "I'm sorry."

Now Bell heard a new arrival enter the house. Owen Randolph's fine voice sounded. "Alice! Are you all right? And you, Missus Drake? What happened here?"

Pete Jennings, his voice deferential, explained to the lawyer.

"Who was the man?" Owen asked.

"Fella named Blackie Fergus," the deputy said. "He's been in Tamarack off an' on for a couple o' years. He had the earmarks of a tough hand. The pushin' kind. Always tryin' to crowd peaceful citizens around. An' so he's dead."

"And good riddance," Owen said. "Do you know anything about him, Irons?"

"I can't rightly figure why he took it on himself to shoot me on account of a little trouble that happened a long time ago," Irons said. "People out there in the street told me this fellow took a job as a rider at Spearhead a few weeks back. Leach Valentine hired him. Maybe Leach or someone out there can find out something about him that'll give me some idea as to why he decided to throw down on me."

Presently they all went away, and the house and the street quieted. Alice came up the stairs and into the room. There was a thoughtful look in her eyes. A new gravity had come upon her. And, contradictorily, Bell sensed there was also a deep and stirring animation within her.

"How many more men has Clay Irons killed?" she asked suddenly.

Bell studied her. "None that didn't need killing, if I read him right," he said.

She smiled then and gave him another of her quick kisses on the cheek and went away. Nancy watched this. Then she, too, left. Soon they had all turned in for the night. But Bell lay awake a long time, still trying to piece the puzzle together—and failing.

He began to chafe at inactivity the next day, but Nancy and Teresa Drake, almost by main force at times, prevailed on him to confine himself to smoking and reading copies of old newspapers and magazines.

The only break in the monotony came late in the afternoon when Owen Randolph escorted Alice home from the office and sat in the parlor for a short time, sipping a cup of coffee and chatting with her mother. During that visit Bell and Nancy remained very quiet above stairs.

Bell awakened the following morning impatient of further restraint. He was still in some pain, but his strength and vigor were returning.

He ate the hearty breakfast Teresa Drake set before him and tried to wheedle her out of more. "I declare," she said, pleased at seeing her cooking appreciated, "you act like you haven't had a square meal in weeks."

"Next," he said, "I'd be the happiest man alive if you'd fetch me my clothes."

"Nancy and Alice told me not to," she protested.

"I may be outnumbered," he said grimly. "But, pants or no pants, I'm getting out of here."

"Not until dark at least," Nancy said.

"That's a deal," he said. "I'll twiddle my thumbs until dark. Now give me my pants. And if there's any more pancake batter . . . ?" He eyed Teresa Drake appealingly.

Afterward, when they were alone, Nancy said: "I wouldn't consent to letting you leave so soon unless I was sure it was for the best."

"Because of what Irons said about somebody else being able to figure out that you had brought me here?"

"Yes," she said. She sat, her head tilted, her lips pursed in a thoughtful manner that he was beginning to find interesting to watch. "Alice says Clay Irons hasn't been able to learn a thing about Blackie Fergus," she went on musingly. "I wonder if that attempt on Clay's life had anything to do with things that have happened to you and me?"

"I've been wondering the same thing," Bell admitted.

"There must be more back of this than old grudges," she said. "Something big. Something we know nothing about."

"I've got the same feeling that all this ties in together," he said. "It's like sitting on dynamite, knowing the fuse is lighted. But you can't find the fuse."

Nancy went to the other bedroom and returned with her handbag that Irons had brought from Marleyville. She drew out the letter her grandfather had written many weeks ago.

Bell read it, then went over it again. " '. . . Leaving everything I possess to you without qualifications . . . ,' " he muttered aloud. He looked up at her, frowning.

"That letter was written the day before the date of his will," she said. "I wonder what caused him to change his mind in so short a time and add the provision that I marry quickly and marry a resident of Minaret Basin?"

"Does Owen know about this?" Bell asked slowly.

"No." She hesitated, then said: "I intended to show it to him, but decided against it after he asked me to marry him."

"Marry him? Owen?"

"He called at the Mountain House that night only a few moments after you had rejected my first proposal," she said. "I'm afraid I laughed at him. He was angry when he left."

"How about Irons?" he asked. "Have you told him about this letter?"

"Irons? No. Why should I?"

"Maybe he knows more about things that are happening to us than we know ourselves."

"Do you think I should tell him about the letter? Do you trust him that much?"

They looked at each other for a long time. "I know," he said wearily. "We're both thinking the same thing. I've gone over it time after time. Irons could have done it all. He could have fired that shot at your window. And pitched my cattle into the river. And he was in Marleyville the night I was hit in the ambush at Durkin's house. He's been around whenever anything has happened."

"And he has also warned you that others are out to kill you," she said steadily. "The other night he as much as warned you against Spearhead and people from Spearhead. Blackie Fergus was working for Spearhead." She stopped, gazing at him challengingly. "I'm from Spearhead, also."

She was trying to be casual. She was stuffing the letter back in her handbag. Another paper dropped to the floor. It was their wedding license.

She realized he had seen it. Tears suddenly began to flow. "I'll have it annulled as soon as possible," she blubbered. "Damn it! Why am I crying? I suppose a person is supposed to cry over weddings."

She rushed from the room and did not return until noon when she brought a tray of food.

"The arrangements have all been made," she informed Bell. "Latigo Jim has left for the ranch with the surrey, unfortunately, so we'll have to depend on a livery rig. Jenny Walking Elk is still in town and Teresa Drake got in touch with her this morning. Jenny often hires a rig to visit her son and his family down the basin. I'll have her rent a surrey and team on that pretense and leave town this afternoon. After dark she'll leave the rig in a vacant lot down the street a short distance from this house. Jenny believes it is a part of our trying to avoid attention because of our marriage." Then she sat, her head tilted in that thoughtful manner. "Where will you go?" she asked.

"To E Loop," he said. "My ranch."

"If anyone is looking for you, he will be sure to go there first," she said. "You can't afford to be seen by anyone until your wound is healed. Jim Hennessy's had a chance to do some thinking by this time and probably has put you on the list of suspects already. There's Spearhead, of course. But they'll look there, also."

"What other people know and what we know are entirely different matters," he said. "The money you gave me is in a drawer in the dresser. It's yours. But Spearhead is not mine. That was no part of any bargain."

"As you wish," she said, her voice very low.

"You're right, of course," he said wearily. "I've got to hide.

There's a place not far from E Loop. It was an outlaw hide-out in the old days. I haven't been there in years. I doubt if another person alive, except Wilcey Pickens, knows about it. He's the last of the Enright Wild Bunch. Nobody but you and I know that he was once a longrider."

XX

The body of Blackie Fergus was buried in Tamarack's small graveyard that afternoon before sundown. Clay Irons was the only person who followed the hearse out of town. At the bleak cemetery on the bench he helped the Reverend Obadiah Tice and the undertaker carry the coffin to the grave.

Blackie Fergus, in death, seemed to have no friends, and there had been nothing in his pockets to indicate that he had relatives. He had been carrying $100 in gold coins, however. Strangely, according to bartenders Irons had talked to, the man had apparently been flat broke earlier on the day he was killed. Pete Jennings had impounded the money on the possibility heirs might be located later.

Irons was paying for the funeral. He was attending the burial, not for vainglory, but because there was deep within him a hard, God-fearing core of humility. His tall hat in hand he stood looking down at the coffin he had helped lower into the earth, thinking that he was no closer now than he had been when he had held his smoking gun in his hand to knowing why Blackie Fergus had tried to kill him.

The gold money might be the key, but he had spent long hours tracing Fergus's action, and had found no door to open with that key.

He had talked to Leach Valentine and had learned nothing. "I put him on the Spearhead payroll when a couple men quit," Valentine had said. "I don't know where he came from. Maybe some of the other boys can tell you more about him. I've been fired, you know. I suppose Bill Andrews is acting as boss of the crew until that girl makes up her mind about naming a new foreman. Likely it'll be Bell Enright."

Obadiah Tice opened his prayer book, then paused, for a buggy was coming out from town at a fast gait. It was Owen Randolph's rig. It pulled up nearby and Owen helped Alice Drake down. "She insisted on coming," Owen explained, and shrugged as though washing his hands of the responsibility.

Alice stood at Irons's side while the minister read the burial service, then sprinkled the coffin with earth, and confined the mortal remains to the soil and the soul to eternity.

She took Irons's arm and walked to the buggy. "No one should go from the earth so alone and so shunned." She sighed. "May heaven have mercy on him."

"An' on me," Irons said. "It was my hand that sent him into death. An' he was not the first."

"You can't let this stand on your conscience," she protested. "It was forced on you."

"All of 'em were forced on me," he said bitterly.

Owen spoke impatiently. "Come, Alice! I've still got important matters to take care of today."

Irons helped her into the buggy and watched it head back to town. She looked over her shoulder at him, and there was still the soberness of their talk in her expression. Then a warmth came as though something greater than the thought of death had dispelled all the ghosts.

Irons rode into town at a slower pace, arriving at dusk. He stabled his horse at a livery. There were more strangers on the sidewalks and moving in and out of the gambling houses and bars. Wagon and saddle flow was heavier. Another of the portable dance halls was being assembled on Front Street. The town's pulse beat had quickened, but there was uncertainty in its tempo. No real money was being spent. Some of the knockdown establishments had never been unloaded from flat cars that stood on sidings.

Everyone was awaiting announcement of the Mid C's decision on the route to be followed out of the basin. They were ready to swarm in any direction with the payrolls of the construction crews as the lure. Heavy odds were offered that the Clear Fork route had been selected, that Tamarack would soon be abandoned, and that Nancy Carmody would be a millionairess. Property was being offered in Tamarack for the price of a horse with which to carry the seller out of the country.

Irons left the livery and strolled down Main Street. Many eyes followed him. He had let it be known that he knew no more than they did and that Henry Driscoll, president of Mid C, was not in the habit of taking him into his confidence in such matters. Some of them did not believe him.

The afternoon train from Marleyville was arriving. Passengers began to stream into Main Street from the depot. Irons came to attention suddenly, watching a big man wearing a star on his vest. It was Sheriff Jim Hennessy who had just arrived from the county seat. Hennessy moved up the street at the determined pace of a man with pressing business on his mind and entered the building where his deputy, Pete Jennings, presided over the Tamarack office.

Irons rolled a smoke and stood a moment, as though idling the time. Clear nightfall was pushing the last glow of day out of the sky and Minaret Peak stood in its cape of snow against the dark azure background. All of this beauty sent Irons's thoughts back to Alice Drake.

At length he crossed the street and strolled past the deputy's office. Hennessy and Pete Jennings were in earnest talk. Leach Valentine and the black-jowled Shep Murdock sat, waiting at a table in the corner, cards and poker chips scattered before them.

Irons went on by without changing stride and entered the Nugget Restaurant. Breaking his usual strict habit, he took a table at the front where he was visible to passers-by, but also where he had a view of Pete Jennings's office. He ordered a meal and ate leisurely, finishing off with coffee and a cigar. That required more than an hour.

Then he remembered there was also a rear door in Jennings's office that opened onto a small corral and stable the county maintained for its Tamarack enforcement office. He at once paid for his meal and left the Nugget and walked past the county office. It was vacant. A lamp still burned there, but the street door was locked.

Irons's stride lengthened. He covered the two blocks westward to Buffalo Street in a hurry. Swinging into this thoroughfare, he advanced a block, then broke into a run.

The Drake residence was in the middle of the next block of scattered dwellings. Several saddle horses stood massed in the darkness before that house.

As Irons neared the scene, the front door opened and Sheriff Hennessy and Pete Jennings stepped out onto the porch and stood in the lamplight. Leach Valentine and Shep Murdock came from the rear of the house and into the front yard.

Alice and her mother were standing in the lighted parlor. Irons heard Jim Hennessy say: "Sorry, ladies. An' thank you for co-operatin' with us."

The two officers came down the steps and through the gate. Irons halted them. "What's this all about?" he demanded.

Jim Hennessy peered. "Oh, howdy, Clay," he said, his manner shifting from gruffness to friendliness.

"What are you doin' here, Jim?" Irons asked. "The Drakes are acquaintances of mine." There was a thread of metal in his voice.

"Sure, sure," Hennessy said uneasily. "I'll tell you about it."

He lifted his hat to Alice and her mother. "Again I thank you, ladies," he said. "And apologies."

"I can't say that you were welcome, Jim Hennessy!" Teresa Drake snapped. "The idea . . . coming here with a search warrant as if we were criminals!"

Irons fancied that her right eyelid drooped just a trifle as she glanced at him. Teresa Drake was finding a heady excitement in the hazardous situation into which she had been drawn. Then she closed the door.

Irons walked with the sheriff to the sidewalk. "I'll take you into my confidence, Clay," Hennessy said. "We know now who killed Sid Durkin."

"Who was it?"

"Bell Enright," Hennessy whispered. "I should have guessed it right at the start, being as he's already served one jolt for harborin' one of his father's old owlhoot pals. I've learned that Matt Barker was another of the Wild Bunch."

"But Enright was married only a few hours before . . . ," Irons began scoffingly.

"That's what threw me off," Hennessy said. "I had no reason to link him with it. I figgered he had gone off with the Carmody gal on a honeymoon. But Leach here thinks that wasn't a real weddin' at all. Only a ceremony to let her inherit Spearhead. Enright grabbed at the chance to use that as a blind for bein' in Marleyville to help Barker git out of jail."

"You're only guessing," Irons said.

"Show Clay that piece of writin', Pete."

Jennings drew from his pocket a slip of paper. Hennessy struck a match for light. Irons peered at the penciled message that was scrawled in a hand that was obviously disguised.

Depity Jennins

If yer inturested in findin who kilt Sid Deerkin an Mat

165

Barrker it was Bell Enrite If you kin ketch him quick yewll find hes got a bullet in him from the fite. mabbe yewll find him hid at Alice Draks house. They wuz sweet on each other. The Drake home reeks with ciguret smok

There was no signature.

"I found it on my desk this morning," Jennings said, truculent under Irons's stare. "So I wired Jim to come over from Marleyville."

"And on the strength of this you had the gall to search the Drake house?" Irons snorted.

"I had a warrant," Hennessy growled.

"An' what did you find?"

"Nothin'," Hennessy admitted. "But somebody had been smoking cigarettes in that house lately."

Irons laughed jeeringly. "Maybe Missus Drake smokes."

Hennessy whirled angrily, stepped into the stirrup, and pulled his bulk into the saddle. "Come on, boys," he said.

"Where you headin'?" Irons asked.

"I'll pick up a few men to deputize an' ride out to Enright's place. If we ketch him at home, an' he's really the man we want, I'll likely need help. You want to join up, Clay?"

"Not me," Irons said. "I reckon Enright would have cause to come up smokin' if a bunch of riders moved in on his ranch house in the late hours of the night."

"We can build some smoke ourselves," Hennessy said. "All I'll ask of him is to prove he's not carrying any fresh bullets in his carcass. If he can do that, then the drinks are on me. If not, then he's goin' to have a hard time explainin' his way out of a hang rope."

Irons watched them ride off toward the center of town. He then walked to the door of the Drake home and rang the bell. It was some time before Teresa Drake called: "Who is it?"

When Irons identified himself, the door opened. She

motioned him in and swiftly closed the portal. He saw that she was clutching a cocked .45. He took it from her and carefully lowered the hammer. "You might shoot yourself with that thing," he chided. Then he lowered his voice. "Where are Enright and Miss Carmody?"

Teresa Drake smiled tightly. "You knew Bell was here right from the start, didn't you? Thanks to your warning that other folks might guess it, too, they got away just in time. They pulled out more than an hour before Hennessy came here."

"Where were they headed?"

She inspected him keenly. "If I told you, what would you do?" she demanded.

"Try and find 'em to warn 'em a posse is on the way to E Loop."

"Good! I figured you that way. But Alice is already hurrying to do just that."

"Alice?"

"She didn't waste any time after the sheriff left." Teresa Drake nodded. "She went out the back way a couple of minutes ago, wearing a pair of britches under her skirt for riding. She's on her way to her dad's wagon yards to borrow one of his saddle horses so she can overtake Bell and Nancy."

Irons was startled. But he paused a moment longer. "Tell me! Were there any visitors at your house yesterday while Bell and Nancy were upstairs?"

"Visitors? Let me think. A tin peddler came to the door, but I didn't buy anything. And a boy from Lowery's general store with groceries. Then, of course, there was Owen Randolph who brought Alice home from the office yesterday and from the funeral today. He sat in the parlor and drank coffee. None of them got far enough into the house to suspect anything. Bell and Miss Nancy were as quiet as mice and . . ."

She was talking now only to herself. Irons was leaving by way of the rear door also, moving at long, desperate strides. "Jupiter!" he was gasping. "They'll all be killed! Alice, too!"

She watched him race off southward through a vacant lot and into the dark street. Her husband's wagon yards and corrals were located on the fringe of town in that direction.

XXI

Nancy drove the surrey and Bell tried to make himself comfortable in the back seat. He had on a heavy weather coat and Nancy wore breeches, a woolen shirt, and a duck jacket that had been provided from the wardrobe in the Drake household.

All the storm curtains in the surrey were in place and tightly buttoned. Behind them, as the vehicle ascended the bench westward, the lights of Tamarack turned a pale yellow, twinkling in the distance.

The rugged flanks of Minaret Peak drew nearer, with the moon dimly revealing the high snow fields. Here on the bench only scant traces of snow now remained.

Bell folded and unfolded his legs, trying to accommodate his length to the confines of the surrey. The vehicle had seen many years of hard service and sagged rheumatically on its springs. His wound throbbed and every chuckhole beneath the wheels took its toll. He burned with thirst, but in the hurry of their departure a canteen had been forgotten, although Teresa Drake had seen to it that a well-filled gunny sack of food and camp equipment was in the surrey, along with blankets and quilts.

Nancy turned often to peer at him in the darkness. "Are you all right?" she asked repeatedly.

"Fine," Bell would reply each time.

The team of roans, like the surrey, had seen better days, and, although the animals were sound of wind and limb, they were heavy-footed and utterly opposed to this nocturnal trip. Their opposition became a trial to Nancy. "You double-damned loaf-ers!" she exclaimed, using the whip, and finally giving vent to a few other vigorous remarks.

"You must have hung around too many camp cooks and muleskinners when you were a button," Bell observed critically.

The pace increased. He gritted his teeth and clung to the struts to ease the worst of the jolting. She caught him at that. With a cry of contrition she at once slowed the horses. "Me and my impatience," she breathed. "Why didn't you tell me?"

"Keep moving," he commanded. "The quicker we get off this main trail the better. We've been lucky in not meeting anybody even this far."

The lights of town finally sank into the blackness of the land astern. Their route swung higher, followed the base of the mountain, then veered to the north. They passed through a thick stand of timber as the roans began bucking the increasing slant of the climb to the Boiling Fork divide.

Presently they encountered a rider bound for town. They answered his jovial greeting, but, when he pulled up for the customary trail chat, they drove on past, hidden behind the shelter of their storm curtains.

"From the Rafter K up Round Valley way," Bell said. "I made out the brand. He's on his way to Tamarack to blow in his pay."

After another fifteen minutes they reached their first mountain stream in a brushy draw where frost lay white on grass and deadfalls in the dappled moonlight. Bell slumped on his face at the brink of a shallow dip and let himself savor the icy coldness of the water on his dry lips and feverish throat.

Nancy placed a hand on his forehead. "We should have kept you in bed another day or two." She sighed.

They straightened abruptly as they heard the rumble of fast-moving hoofs. They looked at each other in consternation. Rid-ers were coming up the trail at a lope and it was too late to attempt to move the surrey out of sight or even to seek cover for themselves.

Two mounted persons, following the road, came down through the brush and into the open moonlight at the ford. Bell was standing, six-shooter in hand. He lowered it suddenly, and then pushed it back into his belt.

It was Nancy who spoke. "Alice!" And then in a different and waiting tone: "And you, Clay!"

The horses steamed in the chill mountain night and gulped for air. "Better get that rig out of here an' into hidin' somewhere as fast as possible," Irons spoke. "Jim Hennessy an' a posse aren't many minutes behind us. They're after you, Bell."

Bell scowled at Alice. "And why are you here?"

"It was a pretty night for a gallop," she said waspishly. "And you're wasting precious time standing there, glaring at me."

Bell and Nancy scrambled into the surrey. She pulled the horses away from the water they were nuzzling and popped the whip. They bounced across the ford and out of the creek bottom into an open flat where scattered sagebrush grew.

The ancient roans soon began to falter. Bell peered around, then pointed to his right. "There, off trail and uphill," he said. "To the far side of that bunch of aspen. Those quakies are thick enough to hide us."

The surrey skidded off the road onto the loose soil of the mountainside and circled a stand of quaking aspen that grew in a characteristic compact clump amid the sagebrush. Alice and Irons followed.

Sheltered from the trail, Nancy pulled up. Alice and Irons slid to the ground. Alice tottered on stiffened legs and clung to him. "That's what comes of growing up," she chattered. "I used to ride bareback all day and never knew what it was to have a stiff muscle. Now look at me. Soft as jelly. Why I haven't been on a horse in a year or more."

Irons shook her gently and said: "That's the first time I knew they made jelly out of grit an' spunk."

Bell climbed out of the surrey. "Who's with Hennessy?" he asked.

"Leach Valentine an' Shep Murdock, among others," Irons said. "Does that sound familiar?"

"They searched our house for you not long after you and Nancy had left," Alice said. "I was saddling a horse at Dad's stables afterward, intending to overtake you and warn you, when Clay showed up."

"Seems like someone wrote a note to Pete Jennings sayin' you are the man who shot that jailer in Marleyville," Irons stated. "The note said they'd likely find you hidin' in the Drake house because you an' Alice were sweethearts."

"Cherchez la femme," Nancy said.

"I read the note myself," Irons went on. "Jim Hennessy showed it to me. Someone had tried mighty hard to appear ignorant an' illiterate. Too hard."

"Whoever it was seems pretty good at guessing," Bell said.

"This fellow wasn't guessin'." Irons shrugged. "Sometimes a man can sell his life just for the sake of a smoke. Tobacco smoke lingers in a house. It's easily detected by a man who doesn't smoke any himself."

Alice uttered a startled gasp. "Good heavens! Clay, are you trying to say that . . . ?"

Bell lifted a warning hand. "We weren't far ahead of 'em at that," he murmured.

Riders were coming. He and the others stood rigidly aware of the imminence of danger. Their covert was little more than 100 yards from the road.

"They're headin' for your ranch," Irons murmured. "That closes it to you. In case we should have to split up an' I'd want to get in touch with you, is there any particular place I might have any luck?"

"Why do you keep wading deeper into this?" Bell asked.

Irons shrugged. "I started investigatin' the wreckin' of some cattle cars belongin' to the company I work for," he said. "Remember? That got me in only up to my ankles. Now I'm still wadin' in. But it's all the same job, in my opinion. An' then there's another reason maybe."

Bell stood looking at him, and at Nancy and Alice, weighed by a bleak sense of depression. He alone was responsible for the way they had become enmeshed in his predicament.

"If we separate and you want to locate me, look up Wilcey Pickens," he said. "Tell him I said to bring you to the Pouch. He'll know what I mean. He lives on Sawmill Creek."

"Sounds interestin'," Irons said.

It was dangerous to talk any more, for the riders were now stringing into view on the trail. They came abreast of the aspen thicket, moving at the unchanging pace of men who had a distance to travel. Bell counted six men in the party. He identified Leach Valentine by his flat-crowned, wide-brimmed hat and recognized the heavy, sloping shoulders of Shep Murdock.

The group moved on past. He felt some of the high tautness sift out of him and knew the others were breathing a little easier, also. Then the saddle horse Irons had been riding lifted its head and whickered a loud challenge at those passing animals!

Pete Jennings's burred voice sounded. "Hey! Who's there?"

There was a boil of hoofs as the manhunters swung around.

"Somebody's up there!" Leach Valentine's voice snapped. "There's not likely to be any loose horses on this side of the mountain."

Bell moved first. He reached for the reins of the horse Irons had been riding. But Irons was nearer and had the same thought. "Not with that gouge on your short ribs," the Kentuckian murmured. "You wouldn't last a mile. I'll draw 'em off."

He was in the saddle before Bell could interfere. He raked a spur along the ribs of the horse, which was a powerful sorrel, and the animal was on its way, its shoes striking fire from the small rocks in the soil. Then it was in the open, heading uphill toward the black bulk of the mountain.

"There he goes!" That was Jim Hennessy's bawling voice. "Stop, Enright! Stop, or we'll shoot!"

A six-shooter opened up, its concussion heavy and thunderous as it echoed from timber and boulders. Other guns joined in, their massed explosion an offense to the ears.

The six riders spurred in tumultuous, shouting pursuit of the vague figure that was building up distance away from them.

The rush of hoofs overrode the startled rearing of the two harness horses and the mount Alice had been riding. Bell caught the reins of the roans, curbing them, and was helped by Alice while Nancy quieted the saddle horse.

Jim Hennessy's strident voice sounded again. "Go back there, Pete, an' look around. I'll bet a cigar Nancy Carmody was with him an' is hidin' out in them quakies. Round her up. She's got a lot of explainin' to do."

Bell realized the posse men were unaware a surrey had come up the trail ahead of Irons and Alice. Evidently the lawmen had encountered the townward bound Rafter K rider but had only inquired if he had seen a man and a girl riding up the trail. The cowboy probably had seen no significance in the passing of the surrey and had not mentioned it.

Hennessy had not the least suspicion that Irons and Alice were involved or were within miles of this place. Nancy was equally swift in assaying the situation. She had grasped the saddle horn and had a foot in the stirrup before Bell turned. He uttered an angry protest. "Dammit! No!"

He made a lunging dive as she swung aboard the horse. His

fingertips caught her ankle for an instant, but she wrenched away from him.

Then she was riding, also, sweeping into the open and lashing the horse into greater speed. Bell, sprawled on hands and knees, watched helplessly.

Pete Jennings came galloping by little more than a stone's throw away. He was yelling furiously: "Stop! Stop, Nancy, you fool girl!"

Jennings was a lumpy, heavy-handed rider. He was no help to any horse and his mount was no match for the Morgan-bred animal Nancy was riding. Jennings was having his troubles in the rough going. He bounced past without seeing the surrey and the team in the deep shadows of the aspens.

Nancy drew him steadily away southward in the opposite direction from that taken by Irons. The posse men were shooting at the Kentuckian occasionally. And Jennings was continuing to howl angry demands for Nancy to halt.

All these sounds lessened, and finally died in the night. Bell got to his feet. "By hell's purple fire, I'll spank her until she's pink and red!" he raged.

Alice laughed hysterically. "Now that's an ungrateful attitude. She and Clay saved your stubborn neck for you."

"But why?" he demanded hotly. "They owe me nothing."

"Clay has already told you why he's on your side," she said. "It's part of a job for the railroad that he started out to do. But Nancy . . ." She didn't finish it. She changed the subject. "Now what do we do? Some of them may come back this way."

Bell pointed to the surrey. "You're heading back to Tamarack," he said grimly.

"And sit stewing at home worrying about you and Nancy and . . . and Clay?"

"Stew or fry. That's where you're going."

"Oh, no, I'm not," she stated positively. "And let's have none of your threats of spanking. My mind is made up."

Bell could not budge her. Submitting to her will in the matter, he climbed into the surrey. He permitted her to handle the reins, but he occupied the front seat with her, the pistol gripped in his hands.

He strained his eyes and ears for sight or sound of danger as they returned to the trail and pushed along its wheel ruts again. But nothing came back from the distances into which Irons and Nancy and their pursuers had gone.

After a mile he said: "There to the left. Bear off on that old logging road."

The route was an overgrown, fading wheel track that had not been used by vehicles in years.

XXII

The country grew wilder. The surrey often teetered drunkenly on slants as it edged past washouts. Brush and tree branches clawed at the surrey curtains. On one occasion a dark, snuffling shape fled from the thicket and went crashing noisily down the mountainside. "Grizzly," Bell murmured. "Lucky he didn't feel in the mood for combat. He's likely lean and hungry after a winter in a den. I know how he feels. All I can do is keep running, also."

He told Alice the whole story—about the letter from Matt Barker, the loss of his cattle, the gun trap at Durkin's, and his flight with Nancy. "And so she brought me to your house for safekeeping," he concluded. "She thinks that as long as she's legally my wife she's got to stand by me."

Alice suddenly leaned over and kissed him on the cheek. "I believe I know how she feels," she said.

The roans halted as they came to a spot where the road had been wiped out by an avalanche that had torn a gouge in the mountainside. This was the end of the trail for the surrey.

"Bareback," Bell said. "You'll now have the pleasure of reviving those memories of childhood you mentioned."

"It will be no pleasure at my advanced age," Alice admitted. "But I'll get along. I'm dubious about you, however."

"I'll yell calf rope when I've had enough," he said.

They unharnessed the roans and rode them, equipped only with halters and carrying the food sack and the quilts and blankets. Bell saw by the position of the moon that it was now past midnight. The roans were tiring.

They topped the divide at last. Dropping away before them lay the valley of the Boiling Fork. Minaret Peak was now slightly southwest of them. Directly west the faint shapes of the lower, but rough and gorge-cut Red Mountains towered in the moonlight. Nearer at hand loomed Castle Butte whose eastern face was a sheer cliff forming a barrier for nearly ten miles from the toe of the Minaret to the badlands near Round Valley.

The only break in the cliff was made by the Boiling Fork that drained the north slopes of the Minaret and cut through Castle Butte by way of a gloomy, impassable defile known as Roaring Gorge. After emerging from the gorge into the valley, the river hurried for five miles through a series of rapids and small, beaver-dammed meadows. This area formed Bell's E Loop graze. The stream then entered another cañon to the east and finally joined the Clear Fork to form the Minaret River.

This was home to Bell. The busy droning of the Boiling Fork came drifting intermittently over the distance. In daylight the modest log-built house and spread of corrals and hay meadows that Josh Enright had built and where both of them had spent pleasant years would have been visible. But this vista was hidden from view in the darkness.

There was no sanctuary for him there now. Even so, he considered stopping at the ranch, a bitter opposition against retreating any farther boiling up inside him.

Alice guessed what was working in his mind. "You can't fight officers of the law," she spoke anxiously. "Not after everything Nancy and Clay have done to prevent it."

She was right, he realized. Silently he rode on westward toward the massive bulk of Castle Butte, descending gradually into the valley and nearer the river.

The headwaters of the Brulé River, which drained the west slopes of the Minaret and the Reds were scarcely ten miles westward. It was the Brulé Valley the railroad must reach, for it offered an easy route out of the mountains into rich range and wheat country that would boom once it had a railroad outlet to Eastern markets.

But Castle Butte, with its perpendicular eastern face and impassable Roaring Gorge barred the way as far as the Boiling Fork was concerned. Even the top of the butte itself was an impenetrable tangle of fallen timber and thick undergrowth. Fire had ravaged the original stand of big timber before the memory of white men, and the second growth among the labyrinth of huge, fallen trunks had bloomed jungle-thick. It was a lair of wild animals, rattlesnakes, and other crawling things. No person, as far as Bell knew, had ever thought it worth the effort to fight his way through that endless tangle across the face of the butte.

The thin cold of the mountain night gradually worked into their bones. Alice wrapped a quilt about herself and still shivered. Occasionally cattle moved off into the brush around them. These were Bell's own E Loop animals. But their numbers were pitifully few. It had been a losing battle all the way—first his father and then the both of them, and now himself alone—against the opposition of the Minaret people to anything pertaining to the name of Enright.

He suddenly aroused, peering down into the gloom of the

valley. Alice uttered a little cry of anger and protest. They sat watching a tiny red dot form in the distance. That spark grew and blossomed into savage, consuming life. Flames soared high and wild, outlining the tall spires of the timber. His ranch house and stable were burning!

He sat for a long time, watching. Finally he said: "The posse has reached E Loop. There's your law and your justice."

The first gray tinge of dawn now lay upon them. Alice stared at his haggard face in that faint light. "I still say you can't fight the law, no matter what they've done to you," she said desperately. "You'll only be destroyed."

They rode on. Alice studied him anxiously. Finally she said: "Calf rope! I've had enough. I simply can't go another step."

Bell suspected she believed he was the one who needed respite. In any event it was dangerous to travel in daylight. They took cover on a slope amid a tangle of boulders overgrown with young evergreens. Bell stretched blankets and quilt and they drank from a small stream that seeped through the brush. "A Siwash camp," he said. "Fresh air, fresh water, and the sky for a ceiling."

Alice insisted on taking a look at his injury. "At least it's no worse," she said. "Ulysses Sylvester was right. He said you were as healthy as a young bear."

They ate a cold meal and slept side-by-side until past noon. Bell awakened many times, his nerves tuned to cry an alarm at the slightest sound. Once it was the rattle of falling bark from a dead fir, dislodged by a jay. On another occasion it was the bumbling panic of a snowshoe rabbit that had blundered almost upon their blanket-wrapped forms before stampeding. Finally it was a new intrusion that brought him sitting tensely upright.

He lifted the pistol and thumbed back the hammer. Something or someone was in the brush beyond a boulder a few rods away. Alice aroused and crept close, pressing tightly against him.

Then Bell lowered the weapon. A slim figure stepped from cover and came hurrying toward them. It was Nancy. Alice hastily moved away from him.

Seeing this, Nancy forced a bright and molded expression of approval into her face. "I hoped it might be you two, but I had to creep nearer to make sure!" she exclaimed. "Alice, you seem to have taken good care of him."

Nancy had lost her bonnet and had arranged her hair in two braids that hung down her back. Her breeches and saddle jacket were mud-spattered and wrinkled. There were marks of fatigue and strain about her eyes and mouth.

"I gave Pete Jennings the slip last night after letting him keep me in sight for a couple of miles," she said. "I took cover in the brush not far from here before daylight. I nearly froze, but finally fell asleep after the sun had warmed things up. I had started out again when I heard your horses moving in the brush."

Bell glared at her. "Why did you come back? Why didn't you head for . . . ?" His voice trailed off.

"Exactly." She shrugged. "Where would I go? Tamarack? Spearhead? Jim Hennessy and Jennings hope that I would do just that. I'm not ready to answer any of their questions. I remembered what you told Clay Irons. I know where Wilcey Pickens's cabin is on Sawmill Creek. I used to explore this Boiling Fork country when I was a young girl. I decided I'd try to get in touch with him and ask him to lead me to this place you mentioned, the Pouch. But first, I came in this direction in the hope I might run into you. It was a lucky hunch." Then she smiled a trifle wanly. "I've got to find a hide-out, too, you know. There's nothing else I can do until . . ."

"Until what?" Bell asked.

"Until all this is settled one way or another."

He sat staring bleakly into the distance for a time. "Maybe the only way it'll ever be settled is for me to get out of the country," he said.

"That might be best," she said reluctantly. "I feel that you'd never live to go to trial if they catch you."

"If I pulled out, what about you?"

"I imagine I would return East, or perhaps go back to Europe. They wouldn't follow me there."

"What about Spearhead?"

She was silent for a time. "I'm not sure what I want to do about Spearhead. I can't feel anything about Spearhead until . . . until I also feel that I really own it."

"What do you mean . . . until you feel that you really own it? You do own it now that . . . now that . . ." He began to flounder.

"Exactly," she said wearily. "Now that I've gone through a marriage ceremony. But that was a subterfuge. An unholy alliance, some people would call it. You needed money to buy the escape of a man accused of murder. I acquired ownership of a valuable ranch. None of the real things that marriage is supposed to mean was included in our transaction. I'll never feel that I qualified for owner of Spearhead under those terms."

"This will that your grandfather left?" he asked. "Did you read it yourself? Did you see the signature?"

"Yes. But I can't say I looked it over with the thought there might be something wrong about it."

"Do you believe now there was something wrong with it?"

"You read Grandfather's letter. What do you think?"

"That the will could stand some close looking over." He nodded.

"That can be done at any time," she said. "Mister Randolph still has it in his safe, no doubt."

"No doubt," he said thoughtfully. "You never intended to keep Spearhead for yourself as long as you had to get control of it by this skullduggery as you regard it, did you?"

"No," she admitted, and once again she was suddenly on the verge of grief. "I . . . I'll turn it over to charity, I suppose. I'll have the right, at least, to name the men who administer it. My . . . my conscience wouldn't let me keep it the way . . . the way things are now. Oh, yes, I do have a conscience, even though you do not believe it."

She was near exhaustion. Bell suddenly picked her up in his arms as he had the day he had carried her across the muddy street in Marleyville, and placed her on the blankets. "Right now what you need is rest and food," he said.

He sat there on his heels a moment longer, looking down at her. "You have a conscience." He nodded. "And a few other items I'll tell you about someday."

"You've at last said something she might want to hear," Alice told him, and began pulling off Nancy's boots. "Go away now until I tuck her in. She's about beaten out."

XXIII

The search for them continued relentlessly. While Nancy slept during the afternoon, Bell kept watch. Twice he sighted riders along the river. Pete Jennings and another posse man passed by a short rifle shot from their hiding place in the thickets. Later in the day Bell glimpsed all these men moving eastward toward the lower gorge below E Loop range. The word evidently had gone out to shift the search in that direction.

He deemed it safe to travel two hours before sundown. They retrieved Nancy's horse, which she had left in the brush a short distance away, and the three of them pushed westward again, keeping to cover. As they advanced, the massive barrier of Castle Butte loomed higher and higher in the foreground, shutting off the dome of the sky.

At early twilight they emerged on the floor of the valley at the margin of the Boiling Fork. The river at this point was a wild chaos of white water, tumbling over boulders and rock ledges. Now they had a clear view into the break in the butte that was Roaring Gorge. Shadows were lilac in hue there, and then began deepening into somber purple masses in the depths of the defile. Buttresses of sheer rock rose 500 feet or more into the red-gold sky.

Moving upstream, they soon left the rapids behind. Directly below the portals of the gorge the river widened into a great, circling pool where flecks of foam formed on the spinning glass-green eddies. Bell watched a sizeable snag of driftwood come into the pool on the river's current and be snatched downward into the vortex.

He kept the horses moving fetlock deep along the margin of this sand-bottomed pool. The girls sat straighter and straighter in the saddle, staring, for they were advancing steadily toward the gorge itself.

A small side creek entered the main river from the south and the horses splashed across its mouth. "If they track us this far, they'll figure we bottom-walked that pup creek back into the mountains to cool our trail," he said. "There's no other reasonable thing for them to think."

They stood finally in the mighty jaws of the gorge itself. They were now racing the deepening dusk. The cliffs soared spectacularly above them. The river's damp tang mingled with the chill of the dying day. There was no wind and the brush and small pines that clung to crevices in the great rock walls were like folds of drapery. In the valley behind them the deep silence of the timber was accentuated by the hushed grumbling of a squirrel and the muted whispering of the river.

They had a full and fearsome view into the purple gorge. The river came sliding from its depths like an endless, great ribbon of gray steel. The defile seemed filled from wall to wall with the rush of the stream.

Bell knotted together the three hackamore ropes and stretched it between them. "Keep close up," he said. "If anything happens, hang on to the rope and don't try to save the horses."

"We're . . . we're going in there?" Nancy asked.

"It's risky only as far as that shoulder a hundred feet ahead," Bell answered. "There are shelves of solid rock against this wall and there's one under water that's wide enough for a horse. The river's high now with the thaw coming down off big Minaret. Otherwise, we'd walk in dry shod."

Dismounting knee deep in the icy water, he led his horse forward. The animal resisted, tossing its head in fear, but it gained confidence as he talked soothingly and finally suffered itself to be drawn along. The other two mounts followed.

The girls sat, stiff with apprehension. They knew that, if they were to be caught in that steely ribbon of water brawling past them, they would be carried into the undercurrents of the pool, and then onward into the rapids below.

Now there was no turning back. They were moving into the gorge, edging along the wall. The horses still found firm footing, although they were belly deep at times. An eddy helped, for its force was upstream and held them against the wall. Stirrups brushed the wet stone.

The cliffs seemed to crouch threateningly above them. The effect was of advancing into an immense and empty cathedral peopled only by phantoms and the echoes of their whispers.

"A place for angels," Nancy breathed.

"Or demons," Alice said in a shaky voice. "May heaven watch over us now."

Bell stumbled once, and instantly the eddy built its weight against him, threatening to sweep him away from the wall, but Nancy drew him back to safety with the aid of the line.

"Angels," he said. "They've driven out all the ghosts from the old days . . . and the demons, too."

He reached the shoulder, rounded it, and the horses followed. The girls drew long, grateful sighs. Before them now stretched a dry and curving shore of smooth, weather-worn rock. The walls of the cliff swung gracefully to the water's edge, leaving a slanting apron above the river's margin.

This shore and also the cliffs on both sides of the river were pitted with pothole openings where softer rock had worn away during the ages. These ranged in size from tiny apertures that offered nesting places for swallows to great, arched, cavernous alcoves.

The horses emerged from the river onto the sweep of the curving bedrock. Bell emptied his boots and mounted, still dripping. "We'll be there in ten minutes or less," he said.

The horses clumped along the shore for a distance, then he turned them directly into one of the large, arched openings. This one pierced the base of the main cliff. However, the wall above it only ascended some fifty or sixty feet and then came a definite break in which full-grown trees had found root.

"This hole goes on through beneath this break," he said. "Don't get jittery. It's been years since I was here as a boy, but it looks the same as ever. It's only a whoop and a holler to the other end."

The horses balked. He nodded to the girls to dismount and lead their animals. They moved into the tunnel-like opening and for a moment seemed to be confronted only by the blank darkness of a cave. Then they became aware of the steady flow of air around them, and finally saw the faint promise of the fading twilight ahead. The horses' hoofs crunched gravel and sand in a tiny stream underfoot.

After a few minutes Bell pushed aside willows and young pines, and they emerged into the open again. They had to fight their way through this growth for 100 yards or more before emerging into clearer ground.

The girls looked around. They were in a small and gloomy hole in the butte, enclosed by broken and cracked rock walls that rose sheer for 300 feet or more, then slanted away in a series of eroded ledges to the high top of the butte.

"The Pouch," Bell said. "It's not what you'd call cheerful, but the Enright Wild Bunch was glad to look upon it as home at times when things got hot outside."

"But . . . but . . . !" Nancy began, gazing wonderingly around.

"A Gros Ventre Sioux, for whom he had done a favor, showed this place to my father when he was a young man," Bell said. "It's evidently a side draw that once was a pocket opening into the main gorge where the river runs, but this one became blocked by a rock slide. The little stream was the clue that led to that passageway."

"Could this be a part of Split Gorge?" Nancy asked.

Bell shook his head. "Hardly. The Pouch extends only a little way farther . . . not more than a quarter of a mile. But Split Gorge is on the other side of the Red Mountain divide and drops westward into the Butte River country. Its upper end must be all of five miles from here."

"When you mentioned the name of this place, it rang a bell in my mind," she said. "I recall that, when I was about fourteen, I insisted on trying to explore Castle Butte. I had heard stories of how impenetrable it was because of the old burn and the deadfalls and brush. I tried and, of course, found that those stories were not a bit exaggerated. I never got near the top. Poor Jenny Walking Elk and her son, who wasn't married then, had to go along to see that I didn't break my silly neck. I remember Jenny saying afterward that there once had been an ancient Indian trail that nobody used any more from the Brulé right through the Reds and Castle Butte into the Boiling Fork. She said she had gone over it as a small child with her people and that they went by way of what we call Split Gorge and a place called La Poche, which, I'm sure, is the name some of the early French trappers probably gave this place . . . the pocket, or pouch."

Bell stood frowning. "It doesn't seem reasonable, but, then, anything might be possible," he said.

"Right now," Alice said, "there are far more pressing matters to think about than old Indian trails. Food for one. And a place to rest our weary frames."

They rode ahead and soon they saw the outline of a habitation. It was a rude, pole-built shack. "This was where the outlaws lived the riotous life of ease and revelry they talk about," Bell commented. "With none of the comforts of home and civilization . . . but with none of its disadvantages, either."

"You say Wilcey Pickens knows about this place?" Alice asked anxiously. "And can lead Clay here?"

Bell nodded. He was wondering if the Kentuckian might be lying dead somewhere with a posse man's bullet in him. He knew that the same apprehension was in the minds of the girls. But none wanted to voice such a thought aloud.

He walked to the shack, the door of which hung crookedly on a single unbroken strap of cowhide that served as a hinge. "It looks like Wilcey might have been here in the Pouch not too many moons in the past," he said, frowning.

He got a fire going. Teresa Drake had provided cooking utensils as well as food in the gunny sack, and they soon had hot food ready. They ate with keen appetites, sitting in the warmth of the blaze while the stars began to blaze out above the buttes.

"Delicious food," Alice said.

Alice had removed the skirt she had been wearing over her saddle breeches. She was very shapely. Her fair hair hung loosely below her shoulders, for she had been combing it out. Her nose was sunburned and freckles had formed on her cheek bones. She was bright-eyed, bubbling with energy. All the primness had been washed out of her and she seemed content with the makeshift accommodations.

Nancy was cross-legged by the fire, gazing into its depths, her gray eyes broodingly thoughtful. Her braided pigtails gave her an elfin quality. But, like Alice, there was nothing child-like in the fetching contours of her figure even in the rough garb that she wore.

Bell sat watching her, remembering many things—that moment beside the stream outside of Marleyville when she had prayed for moonlight so that she could care for his injury, the nearness of her on that freezing ride by train to Tamarack, and then the new escape from the manhunters on the mountain.

Her eyes suddenly lifted to him as she became aware of his interest. A smile came fleetingly, softening her lips, lighting her face. It was a little revelation of intimate and treasured thoughts, as of secrets shared between them. Then her gaze turned to Alice. Abruptly all these things were veiled from him and she drew her eyes quickly away. But he saw a rush of color rise into her throat. Then it receded as though some succeeding thought had killed that uplift of spirit. She arose, moved to Alice suddenly, and laid her cheek briefly against her face. Alice looked at her quickly, with that sagacity and perception that is the gift of womankind.

Bell examined the shack more closely. If it had been Wilcey who had visited the Pouch, he must have had company, for the pole frames of the two bunks showed signs of having been strengthened with rawhide thongs. And not too long in the past, he decided. The previous fall, perhaps.

An uneasiness grew in him. Then he reasoned that it surely must have been his father who had been with Wilcey. Josh had told him more than once that, with the possible exception of some old Sioux, he was sure only the three of them knew about the Pouch and its hidden entrance.

Pack rats had been busy in the shack. A lizard, just out of hibernation, went speeding away as he moved about.

He lay puzzling over it after he had wrapped up in a blanket beside the fire. On the opposite side of the blaze Alice and Nancy slept huddled together. They preferred the open rather than to chance the uncertain hazards of the shack and its scurrying inhabitants.

The rising sun was glinting on the rim of the butte when he awakened. He ate the breakfast the girls prepared and found that his wound was now only an aching annoyance. The doubts of the night were subdued by the coming of the strong new day, but presently his uneasiness returned.

"We'll pull out tomorrow," he said suddenly.

"Pull out?" Nancy protested. "But you're safe here."

"I'll come back," he said. "But an outlaw hide-out is no place for you two. Alice can make it back to town at night without being stopped if she's careful on the trail. You, Nancy, can look up Wilcey Pickens. He'll see to it that nobody finds you."

"Alice should go back, of course," Nancy said. "They have no proof that she helped us. But they'll probably be watching Wilcey, also. They know he's your friend. And there are many reasons why it would be better if I stayed here with you." She again gave him and Alice one of her bright and polished smiles. "There can be no scandal in that."

"To make more certain of it I'll stay, also," Alice said demurely. "In fact, I refuse to go back until . . . until I know about Clay. Something might have happened to him."

Bell had also been doing some worrying about Irons. "That might take some time," he said. "If Wilcey is off in the hills setting out traps and bait for loafer wolves, Irons won't be able to get in touch with him."

"I'll wait until we know for sure," Alice declared. And there was no moving her from that decision.

Afterward, Bell wandered about. He discovered the scars of bullets in a birch tree a few rods from the shack. The marks were only slightly blackened by weather and the tree had not started to close over these wounds. He decided they had been inflicted the previous fall.

He followed the line of fire and that brought him to the shack itself. He now saw an empty pistol shell in the earth near the door. It was partly embedded in the winter's residue of earth mould. He picked it up. It was a .38 cartridge!

He stood staring at it, a sudden humming, dizzying rush of emotion whirling through him. He was remembering those two battered objects that Clay Irons had shown him.

Kneeling, he found four more empty cartridges of the same caliber. Someone had sat by the door of the shack and had used the birch tree as a target for idle gun practice. Bell doubted that either his father or Wilcey Pickens would have wasted powder and lead on mere target shooting. More than that, he had never known either of them to own a weapon of that caliber. There was no doubt in his mind now but that someone else had been in the Pouch.

He found Nancy at his side, staring at the weather-corroded shells. "What is it?" she asked anxiously.

He said: "I'm beginning to get some things clearer."

He turned and walked farther up the Pouch, following the small stream through the willow brush until he reached a grassy clearing where he found evidence of another camp. At least four men had been there, Bell estimated, and for several days, although the overgrowth of brush indicated that one full summer had gone by since their visit. Nancy had followed him.

"It looks like the Pouch isn't the secret and safe place I

thought it was," he murmured. He moved ahead a few yards, then called to her: "Come here!"

A lane had been hacked through the brush and trees. They could sight for a considerable distance along this opening. Bell stooped, gazing at a wooden stake driven into the soil. It bore a small circular metal plate on which numbers and alphabetical letters were inscribed in a code.

He and Nancy followed this narrow, axed lane and it brought them to a rock slide that apparently was the end of the Pouch. This lofty slope of shattered boulders seemed to be a part of a high ridge that rose against the skyline as they gazed upward. On a boulder at the base of this jumble of rock were more code numbers in bright yellow paint.

Bell began swiftly scaling the broken rock. He reached the crest much sooner than he expected. In fact, he was scarcely 100 feet above the floor of the Pouch where Nancy stood, watching. He found himself gazing down into another gorge that curved off southwesterly through the heart of the butte.

He realized now that what he was seeing was a continuation of the Pouch. Or rather, that the Pouch was a segment of this longer defile. The rock slide, when viewed from below, had formed an optical illusion. The ridge, of which it had appeared to be a part, was in reality some distance away, and the gorge curved along its base. The heap of shattered rock was a barrier that had fallen sometime in the past to cut off the Pouch and give it the aspect of being a lone pocket in the face of the butte.

He came leaping down from the slide and looked wildly at Nancy. "You were right!" he exclaimed. "Jenny Walking Elk was right! There could have been a trail through here from the Brulé. The Pouch is part of a bigger gorge, and I'll bet a little red apple that it's Split Gorge. There probably is another slide west of here beyond which nobody ever thought it worth while to go, figuring it was the end of the gorge from that direction and all that lay ahead was Castle Butte and that tangle of deadfalls."

"And . . . and these marks?" Nancy breathed.

"Surveyors' inscriptions," he said. "That's why men were camped in the Pouch. My guess is that it was last spring. Now I know. . . ."

He turned, hearing slight movement in the brush nearby. He had expected that it would be Alice. But it was not. Leach Valentine and Shep Murdock stood there! They had cocked six-shooters in their hands.

"Raise your arms, Enright," Valentine said. "High and easy. Don't go for that pistol."

"Let him!" Shep Murdock said in his thick, dry voice. "Let him try for it!"

Bell stood a moment, assaying his chances. There was none. Besides, Nancy would be in the line of fire if gun play started.

Leach Valentine spoke again. "Shep, take his gun. Nancy, don't try to interfere. I'll have to shoot even you to stop him, if you force my hand. He's killed two men already, and I won't take chances on him downing me."

Nancy turned, gazing at Bell, and he saw she was as pale as wax. He had realized at once that Valentine and Murdock meant to kill him at the first opportunity. And she knew it now, also.

Murdock grinned wickedly as he took Bell's pistol. "They'll lynch you for sure, Enright. That is, if you ever live to see Marleyville again."

Valentine eyed the painted code on the boulder and said: "So now you know."

Bell nodded. "So now I know."

XXIV

Valentine motioned with his pistol. "Walk ahead of me, Enright. Nancy, again I warn you not to try to interfere. We're acting as officers of the law. We've been deputized. He's under arrest."

"On what charge?" Bell asked.

Valentine caught Bell's shirt and ripped it from him. He then tore off the bandage and pointed to the healing wound. "Bullet hole!" he said jeeringly. "Now where did you ever pick that up?"

"I shot him," Nancy said. "We had a little spat. You know how it is with married folks."

"You'll have to think up a better yarn than that," Valentine retorted. "The charge is murder. He killed a jailer named Sid Durkin when Durkin tried to break up his attempt to set Matt Barker free. Everybody knows Barker was one of his father's outlaw pals. Durkin was an officer of the law. Get moving now."

Bell began walking in the direction indicated, which was through the brush toward the shack. Both Valentine and Murdock kept their guns trained on his back. Nancy placed herself between him and the weapons.

"You want to give him a chance to make a break for it, don't you?" Valentine said.

Bell realized this was their purpose—to give him an apparent opening that would lure him into an attempt at escape and then shoot him down. He knew Nancy understood this, also, for he discerned the darkening dread in her eyes. She drew away from him and ran ahead. Murdock went lumbering in pursuit and overtook her to keep watch on her.

"Who told you how to get into this place, Leach?" Bell asked.

"An old man with a white beard," Valentine said, and laughed knowingly.

"That's a coincidence," Bell murmured. "I ran into him, too. He told me some things about this place I didn't know."

"For instance?"

"Surveyors have been in the Pouch and Split Gorge," Bell said. "It's a railroad survey, of course. How long have you known about it?"

Valentine laughed again. "Long enough. It happened while you were in the pen. It was a life saver for Mid C. The real reason they quit construction when they reached Tamarack was that they couldn't afford to build on the route by way of Round Valley. The Clear Fork route across Spearhead at the south end of the basin wasn't much better. Henry Driscoll and his Mid C had a bear by the tail. They had built a hundred miles of railroad into a blind alley. Then Josh Enright went to Henry Driscoll and showed him how it could be done."

"It's clear enough, now that I've been hit over the head with it," Bell said wryly. "The Mid C can build by way of the Boiling Fork. Reaching the gorge, they just have to bore a hundred yards or so through the base of the butte and they're in the Pouch. They've only got to worry about a few rock slides and they've got an easy route all the way through the Reds into the Brulé River."

"Perhaps not quite that simple, but it's practical and won't cost half the money the others would have set them back," Valentine said. "Josh Enright acted as guide for the survey. Only Henry Driscoll and two of the top Mid C engineers were along. They came in early last spring, pretending they had gone on a hunting trip. Instead, they spent their time in the Pouch and Split Gorge, estimating construction costs."

"And nobody else knew about this?" Bell asked casually.

Valentine was anxious to display his superior knowledge. He was talking freely, for Nancy and Murdock were out of earshot ahead. "Nobody else but the old man with the white whiskers." He snickered. "Josh Enright gave his promise to Henry Driscoll that he'd never let the cat out of the bag until Mid C announced it. That was so speculators wouldn't grab up land before the railroad could make sure it had clear title to its right of way. He made a verbal agreement to give Mid C the right of way across E Loop as far as the gorge."

"He gave it to Mid C?" Bell questioned.

"All Josh Enright asked was that Henry Driscoll use his influence to get you out of the pen," Valentine answered. "Even so, it took quite a while before Driscoll and the Mid C could make the governor listen. Somebody had even bumped off your old man before he had the pleasure of seeing you out where the both of you could carry on your devilment again."

"Driscoll and the Mid C worked on the governor?" Bell said. "But I understood that it was Owen who . . ." He broke off. He realized now that he was hearing only what a dead man was supposed to hear. Valentine was giving rein to his boastful ego only because he felt sure he was talking to a person who would never live to take advantage of what had been said. "Your knowledge surprises me," he said. "You must be very close to the old white-bearded gentleman."

"I know everything about this deal worth knowing," Valentine said.

"Then you know who killed my father and why?"

Valentine laughed but made no reply.

"Maybe you know who killed Matt Barker," Bell went on. "And Sid Durkin."

Valentine quit laughing. "You're only talking yourself deeper into your grave, my friend," he murmured. "You know as much as I do now. And that's too much for your health."

They now emerged into view of their camp. Alice was scouring the skillet at the margin of the stream. She looked up, then sprang to her feet with a little scream and lifted the skillet in an instinctive attitude of defense.

Valentine was equally dismayed. Evidently he had been unaware that a third person was in the Pouch. He uttered a loud and incredulous oath. "What in hell's blazes are you doing here?" he yelled. Then he began to understand. "You lily-fingered fraud!" he frothed. "You did have him hiding in your bed at your house after all, didn't you?"

Alice was ashen-lipped, but her voice was steady and scornful. "I don't know what you're talking about. If anyone was in my bed lately, I assure you I was not present at the time."

"I knew you two were sweet on each other," Valentine raged, "but I didn't think you had the brazen nerve to go into an outlaw hide-out with him."

"Sand you mean," Nancy spoke. "Alice had plenty of it. I can cite several instances."

"Keep out of this," Valentine snarled at her.

"After all, you're accusing my husband of carrying on with her," Nancy said.

"How did you get here?" Valentine roared at Alice.

"The same way you did, I imagine," she answered grimly. "The real question is how did you know how to get here?"

Shep Murdock's stolid mind had gone to the point by this time. "Why that taffy-haired Susie must have been with 'em right from the start," he growled. "No tellin' which one of 'em we was chasin' the other night on the mountain."

Valentine gazed from face to face and saw that Murdock had hit on the truth. He suddenly became icily calm. "Maybe that wasn't even Enright who busted out of cover when that horse whickered," he said. "If so, who the hell could it have been?"

Nobody answered. Valentine realized nobody was going to answer. He turned, and violently kicked their cooking utensils and the remains of their food supply off into the brush. "Where did you get that grub?" he demanded.

"We looked into the gunny sack and there it was," Bell said. "Like manna from heaven."

Valentine had been trying to drag from them some hint as to whether they had been in touch with any other person. "You'll learn considerably more about heaven before long, my friend," he said thickly. "Or hell, more likely."

All color drained from the faces of the girls. They all knew now that Valentine could not afford to let Bell live. Valentine and Murdock conferred in whispers, and then Murdock went away. He was gone some time. When he returned, he was leading their two horses. Evidently they had left the animals in Roaring Gorge and had entered the Pouch on foot before daybreak.

Murdock next brought in the roans and Alice's mount from where they had been picketed.

"The girls will ride the roans," Valentine said. "We're moving out."

He helped Alice mount and she suddenly struck him in the face with the ends of the reins.

"You'll get worse than that if you try to paw me," Nancy warned, and lithely mounted the other horse.

They prodded Bell aboard the saddle horse, and then lashed his wrists to the horn. Valentine motioned him into the lead and fell in behind him. The girls followed and Murdock brought up the rear.

They moved through the passageway beneath the cliff and made the precarious journey along the submerged shelf of rock and into the open below the mouth of the gorge. It was evident that Valentine had been in the Pouch before and knew the hazards of the path.

They headed down the valley of the Boiling Fork. Bell's burned ranch lay in that direction and also the trail to Tamarack. He and the girls were silent now. And all the while the tension inside him spread like a cancerous growth. He was sure that all that had deterred them from shooting him in the back was the presence of Nancy and Alice. Even so, all they wanted was an excuse, no matter how slim, to justify killing a prisoner accused of murder.

He now discovered that the thongs around his wrists were

loosening. The knots had been carelessly tied by Valentine and he was sure this had been done deliberately in the hope of luring him into making a break to escape. Then they would blast him down. The *ley de fuga*.

At length the grim realization came to him that, even though they were setting a trap for him, and he knew their purpose, it was one he must step into. For, if he refused to go for this bait, there were other ways by which it could be brought about. It would be easy to startle his horse into a sudden run. A furtive jab of the spur by Valentine as their mounts crowded near each other in rough going, the burn of a cigarette, or the lash of a quirt would send the animal into a stampede that could be described later as a dash to escape. And he realized that time was running out for him.

They had left the river now and were cutting across one of its loops, moving along a slope through timber and sizeable boulders. His bonds had now slackened sufficiently to permit him to rip his hands free any moment he chose.

He glanced back. The five of them were strung out in single file in rough going. Nancy followed Valentine, with Alice next in line, and then Murdock.

Their curving course let boulders shut out Murdock from view. Valentine's horse was close at the heels of his mount and it flashed upon him that the blond man had decided this was the time for his own purpose, also. He meant to stampede Bell's horse and then begin shooting.

Bell moved first. He tore his hands free, whirled in the saddle, and struck with his right fist. Valentine managed partly to evade the punch and it only grazed his jaw in a glancing blow. But Bell succeeded in his other purpose. His left hand caught the muzzle of Valentine's six-shooter, and, although its owner resisted so that the sight ripped a furrow in his palm, he managed to wrest it away.

He brought the gun back in a raking side slash, and this time he landed solidly, the barrel slamming Valentine high on the temple. The man sagged dizzily, then pitched from the saddle.

Shep Murdock was cursing wildly. Both Nancy and Alice were swinging their heavy roans, doing their best to block him as he tried to crowd past them among the boulders. Bell did not dare shoot at Murdock for fear of hitting the girls. He kneed his horse around, intending to race to meet his man at closer range, but that maneuver on the slant overbalanced his excited mount and sent it lunging and staggering downhill. It might have recovered, but a clump of brush tripped it, and it went completely over end in a somersault.

Bell leaped clear. Another clump of stiff brush saved him from hard impact, but it bounced him and he landed, sliding in loose soil that was matted with decaying pine needles. He finally righted himself, coming to his knees, breathless and shaken. Murdock had spurred past the girls now and was bearing down on him, gun in hand, waiting a clear chance to start hammering the life out of him with bullets.

Bell tried to shoot but the action in the weapon he held would not respond. The gun was dead—jammed with earth as a result of his spill.

Murdock had him and he saw the man's leathery lips peel back in a snarling grin at that discovery.

Then, from the brush to Murdock's right, a pistol exploded. Murdock's hat was knocked sidewise on his head. Startled, the man pumped a wild and wasted shot at Bell. At the same instant, the unseen marksman fired again. This time Murdock's hat was plucked violently from his head and sent spinning away.

Murdock left the saddle in a floundering leap and reached the shelter of a boulder. Bell also dived for cover. The horses Murdock and Valentine had been riding went crashing away through the brush. Bell's mount got to its feet and trotted uncertainly downhill. Nancy and Alice sent their heavy-footed roans down the slant, also, and out of the reach of their captors.

Silence came. And then Bell glimpsed Murdock and Valentine retreating through the timber in the direction their horses had taken.

After a few moments Bell moved around the thicket from which the shots had come. He looked at the mud-caked, lean, unshaven man who stood there calmly pushing two fresh shells into his .45. "Good pennies turn up, too," he said.

"That's a right nice thing to say." Clay Irons chuckled.

"I think they suspect it was you," Bell said. "That's why they didn't try you on for size. They were afraid it might be too tight a fit."

"Better to let the gentlemen fret about it," Irons said. "That's why I was bashful, an' stayed out of sight. They seemed anxious to give you the law of flight treatment."

"You couldn't have dropped out of the blue sky at a better time. But how?"

"I've been hangin' around all day, waitin' a chance to put in my ante," Irons explained. "I located Wilcey Pickens's shack yesterday, but he wasn't at home. I helped myself to some of his grub an' slept there a while, then came back to the Boilin' Fork to see if I could cut your trail. Instead, I sighted Valentine an' Murdock. They were actin' like men who had somethin' right important on their minds. I followed 'em west along the river an' they finally made a cold camp near Roarin' Gorge. They hit the saddle at daybreak, but I lost 'em near the gorge. Vanished right into thin air. I had a hunch they went into the gorge, but couldn't prove it. So, not havin' any other ideas, I hung around there an' finally a whole parade came out of the river with you in the lead. I've been taggin' along ever since. I was afraid to make a move at the wrong time, for they were only waitin' for a chance to let you have it."

Irons's horse was nearby. He mounted and rounded up Bell's animal, which had suffered no serious damage, and they rode to overtake the girls. Nancy and Alice were awaiting them.

More than ever Nancy seemed elfin and very young and slim, sitting astride the roan. Alice was trying to discipline her hair.

"I'll never think of women as weak again," Bell said.

But, as though to prove otherwise, both girls unexpectedly began weeping big, salt tears. "I'm . . . I'm so glad you're both safe!" Alice blubbered.

Nancy tearfully kissed Irons. She turned to Bell, but there was a sudden restraint in her. She said haltingly: "I'm so glad for . . . for both of you . . . and for Alice." She brushed his cheek with her lips.

A deadness of spirit descended on them. Then Irons gripped Bell's hand. "I'm mighty glad, too," he said. "An' for Alice."

"Where are we going?" Alice asked after a time.

"To Tamarack," Bell said. "We'll keep to cover. We don't want to make it before early dark."

Irons eyed him. "Tamarack's the most dangerous place you could pick right now."

"All I need to prove who killed Josh is one thing," he said. Briefly he told Irons the discovery of the secret of the Pouch and Split Gorge. "It's the same thing I started out with. I know now why he was killed. I want to prove *who* fired the shot."

"Any ideas?"

"Yes. And so have you. So have all of us."

"What do you aim to do about it?"

"Smoke him out," Bell said. "Make him show his hand."

"He's killed once," Irons warned. "He will again."

"I've got to give him that chance," Bell said. "In front of witnesses."

"What good'll it do you if you're in your grave?"

"Look who's telling other people to be careful." Bell snorted.

"Who was it who made a target of himself only the other night?"

Nancy now comprehended what they were talking about. She uttered a horrified gasp. "I . . . I forbid it!" she cried. "It's too dangerous!"

"If anybody can figure out a better way, I'll listen," Bell said. "But it's got to be done at once . . . tonight . . . before he gets suspicious. I've got no urge to die just to prove a point. In fact, I'm a lot more anxious to stay alive than I was a few days ago."

"Yes, I know," she said. "You and Alice."

Bell and Alice looked at each other. Suddenly both were smiling as though they shared a great secret. "There may be other reasons," Bell said.

Keeping to cover, they rode toward Tamarack. At mid-afternoon, far behind them, they glimpsed two men riding double, traveling in the same direction. Valentine and Murdock. They'd lost one of their horses.

Bell said: "We'll be in town an hour, maybe two, ahead of 'em. That'll be a break in our favor."

XXV

Owen Randolph sat alone in his inner office behind locked doors. It was night and nearing nine o'clock. A half-empty whiskey bottle stood on the desk. He had been there for more than two hours. He had found himself shaking a little at times and had got the bottle out of his desk, hoping that a stimulant would overcome this weakness. He was not drunk, but the quivery sensation persisted. It was in his fibers—in his nerves.

Events had not gone the way he had mapped them, but, on the other hand, the general picture was shaping up much as he had originally sketched it in. Nancy Carmody had given him a considerable setback by marrying Bell. At first that had threatened to destroy everything, but his mind was resting easier on that score now. He was already preparing to go into court the instant the thirty-day period of grace was ended and charge there never had been an actual marriage.

He felt sure the court would disinherit her and that Spearhead would come under his and Valentine's control through the trustee-charity provision in the document that had been probated as Buck Carmody's testament. He had in his safe the papers marking the encumbrances on Bell's E Loop which would give him control of the route of the Boiling Fork, and he had the foreclosure ready for filing the instant the obligations came due.

There was only one factor that might still destroy him, and that was Bell himself. He knew that, if Bell lived, there would be an accounting between them sooner or later. He expected momentarily to receive the news that this had been taken care of by Valentine. He had been awaiting this word ever since Bell and Nancy had slipped away from the Drake home ahead of the sheriff. And now more than forty-eight hours had gone by.

Jim Hennessy had returned to Tamarack at noon, saddle stiff and disgruntled. Pete Jennings and other deputized men, including Valentine and Murdock, were still in the Boiling Fork country, continuing the hunt, but the sheriff had been forced to take time out to catch up by telegraph with neglected business in his main office at Marleyville.

Owen had talked to him. "What makes you so certain it's Bell Enright and Nancy Carmody you're chasing?" he had asked. "You say nobody got close enough to them to be sure."

"You're a pretty good friend of Enright's, so I hear," Hennessy had snorted huffily. "And of the Carmody gal, too. You know, and I know it was them, all right."

"But you can't convict Bell on what you think," Owen had argued. "You've got to prove it in court."

"I'll convict Enright if I can show he's carrying a fresh bullet wound," the sheriff said. "If he can give me the slip till it's healed, then I'll have to no case at all. He knows that. But, if I can show that he was wounded, along with other circumstantial evidence against him, I'll send him to the gallows for Sid Durkin's murder."

"I feel sorry for Bell," Owen had sighed.

"You could make yourself mighty unpopular in this range by standing up for him right now," Hennessy had said. "Folks figure he's turned killer."

Hennessy was now catching up on sleep in a room at the Mountain House. Owen felt that his talk had served its purpose, which was to plant firmly in the sheriff's mind the belief that he was Bell's friend and defender.

Owen looked at his watch and lifted the bottle again. Surely things could not have gone wrong again. He and Valentine had been certain they knew Bell's eventual hiding place. He had warned Valentine to wait until others were out of the way before entering the place to make the capture.

There were other factors that weighed on his mind. Alice Drake had been absent from her desk in his office. Her mother had sent word that she was ill, but when he had gone to the house, Teresa Drake had said that her daughter was too indisposed to see him. Owen doubted that Alice was either ill or even at home. In addition, Clay Irons seemed to have dropped out of sight. The deadly speed with which Irons had stopped Blackie Fergus in their gun duel brought a little chill in Owen's stomach each time he thought about it, even though he was sure Irons could have no way of knowing that he was the source of the gold money that had been in the man's pockets.

Owen suddenly set the bottle aside. He had heard careful footsteps at the rear door. Knuckles tapped carefully. He started up from his chair eagerly. It must be Valentine at last.

"Who is it?" he called.

"Bell Enright," came the muted answer. "I need some advice, Owen."

Owen stood entirely motionless for a time. His cultured features were completely hard and calculating. He opened a drawer in his desk and lifted out a pistol. It was a compactly mounted .38 with a black handle and a blue steel muzzle. Holding the gun cocked and behind him, he moved to the door, drew the bolt, and stood ready to shoot as he slowly opened it.

Then he relaxed. Bell's features showed no hostility. He had only the gaunt, haggard, desperate aspect of a man who was near the end of his endurance.

"Come in!" he said. "Come in, Bell."

Bell entered the office, and closed the door. "Nobody saw me, Owen," he said reassuringly.

Owen walked to his desk and sat down, holding the gun ready and out of Bell's sight. "You're alone?" he asked carefully. "Where is Nancy?"

"We separated the night the posse chased us," Bell said. "That marriage didn't count anyway."

"Why did you come here, my boy?" Owen asked in his fine voice. "You know they'll hang you if they catch you."

"It's a business matter," Bell said. "I wanted to pay back the money you lent me the other day."

Owen had expected anything but that. "You have the money . . . the twenty-five hundred dollars?"

"I can get it and be back in less than half an hour," Bell said. "It's at the Drake house. I left it there when I pulled out, after Alice had been kind enough to take care of me for a couple of days. I'm sure Missus Drake will let me get it. I hope you have the lien on the cattle handy so I can tear it up."

"I have it, of course." Owen nodded. "But why this sudden rush, Bell? The lien is safe enough."

"I guess I'm just old-fashioned enough to want to get out of debt when I can," Bell said. "I also intend to pay off the mortgage in a few days. The one Josh placed with you."

"That means you'd have to raise more than seven thousand dollars," Owen said slowly. "Where would you get it?"

"I'll get it," Bell said. "How I get it is neither here or there."

Owen was very proud of his self-control at that moment. Suddenly many questions had been answered for him, and they were all in his favor. He was enormously elated, and there was also a scorn in him for Bell's gullibility. It seemed plain enough to him. Bell had been in the Pouch and had discovered the secret railroad survey. Obviously he still did not suspect that Owen himself was responsible for all his troubles and was only trying to make sure that he had a clear title to E Loop. He was married to the heiress to Spearhead, and Owen assumed that was where he expected to get the bigger sum of money. Still unanswered, however, was the question as to the whereabouts of Valentine and Murdock. Apparently Bell had never encountered them.

None of these reflections was permitted to alter Owen's features. Instead, he adopted an attitude of puzzlement. "You place me in an embarrassing position, Bell. I'll wait here for this money you seem so anxious to hand over to me, and will have the lien ready to turn over to you, as you wish. But, in all fairness, I must warn that, if anything comes up, I will be compelled to deny that this meeting took place."

"I understand." Bell nodded. "Associating with a man accused of murder is hardly the proper thing for a respectable businessman. But, I assure you, your reputation will be as safe in my care as my own life." Bell moved to the door. "Be patient, Owen," he said.

"I trust so," Owen said.

"This may take a little time. I'll have to circle the west end of town to make sure nobody sees me."

Owen nodded. "I'll wait."

XXVI

Bell stepped into the dark alleyway and heard Owen close the door behind him. He moved off down the lane. Taking his time, he presently crossed Main Street on the western fringe of town, and then worked his way back to Buffalo Street.

He moved along this unlighted street, and now his heart began to hammer. He neared the Drake residence. Lamplight burned in an upper bedroom and in the kitchen.

Around him the street was asleep and as silent as a tomb. Duckboards and cinders crunched beneath his feet with what, to him, was the voice of thunder.

He reached the gate in the picket fence. And now, suddenly, he experienced a powerful urge to flee. Never had life seemed to hold as much for him, and never had death seemed as close.

For he knew that, if he was right, death was even now reaching for him. He could almost feel the impact of a bullet in his ribs.

Then many things happened simultaneously. A man shouted urgently: "Bell!" That was Clay Irons's voice.

Bell dived to one side, dropping earthward. A gun *boomed* from the opposite side of the street, the wink of powder flame lighting the scene for an instant. The bullet struck the gate post above him. Then two guns crashed in unison across the way. A vague, dark figure leaped from cover. It was a man wearing a linen duster. He had been crouching back of the same stone wall from which Blackie Fergus had tried to ambush Irons a few nights earlier.

This man vaulted the wall into the street. He was fleeing from the voice and the shots that had startled him an instant before he had fired at Bell. He believed Bell had gone down beneath his bullet and that he had no opposition in that direction. So he ran southward along Buffalo Street.

Bell arose, covered the distance in a few strides, and sent his weight crashing into the man, driving him to the street in a breath-taking fall. Bell scrambled on top of him. His victim tried to swing up the pistol he held, but Bell planted a knee on the gun arm, pinning it down.

"Save your squirming for the hang rope, Owen," he said.

Irons came racing up, followed by Sheriff Jim Hennessy. The door in the Drake home opened. Nancy ran across the porch and to the gate, and stopped there as though fearing what she might see.

"I'm all right!" Bell called. "He missed. You yelled in time, Clay." He stood, looking at Nancy. She remained motionless for a time, gazing at him. He could see the fine outline of her features and the deep shadow of her eyes. She laid a hand on the fence, as though needing support for a moment. Then she turned and joined Alice and Teresa Drake.

Bell took the gun from Owen's limp hand and hoisted the man to his feet. He looked at the weapon, then handed it to Irons, and said: "This clinches it. It's a Thirty-Eight."

Irons hefted the gun. "Owen," he said, "you should have got rid of this thing long ago. I've got two used bullets in my pocket that came from this gun. I'm sure we can prove it when we get you before a murder jury."

Jim Hennessy took charge of their captive. "I'd never have believed it if I hadn't seen it myself, Owen," he said. "I'd never expect a man like you to turn killer. You walked into a trap. Bell Enright baited it with his own life and got away with it."

"This is ridiculous!" Owen gasped, finally finding his voice. "Bell, I was chasing the man who tried to murder you."

"You can't lie your way out of this one, Owen," Bell snapped.

Hennessy led the prisoner into the Drake house, the others

following, and shut the door in the faces of the curious who were beginning to gather. "Enright came to the hotel right after dark to talk to me, Owen," he explained. "Irons was with him. Enright told me the whole story. It took some tellin'. I was mighty hard to convince. Both him an' Irons sorta had to hold me down an' make me listen. Finally some of the things he said began to make sense. He said he was sure he knew who had killed Josh Enright, and that this same man was responsible for other things that had happened. He didn't name you, but said he'd set up a deal to bring this man into the open. Me an' Irons were hunkered out across the street, waitin' for Bell to show up. An' you showed up first."

"You hustled here as soon as I left your office, Owen," Bell said. "You figured you could scuttle safely away after you killed me. With me dead you knew you'd be safe."

"You're insane!" Owen frothed.

"You worked both sides of the street," Bell accused. "You learned that my father had shown the railroad the way through Split Gorge. I have a hunch it was something Josh said in one of the letters you wrote for him to me while I was in prison that tipped you off. I never got that letter, or any other word from Josh about the railroad. You saw to that. And you must have wheedled the whole story out of him and even got him to take you into the Pouch."

"I don't know what you're talking about," Owen snarled.

Bell was doing some guessing, but he and Irons and the girls had gone over the events of the past and he was sure he was very close to being correct in every detail. "You rigged a double-barreled scheme to get rich," he said. "You unloaded everything you owned here in Tamarack at top prices. You knew Buck Carmody wasn't likely to live through the winter. You were his lawyer and had drawn up his will, which left everything to Nancy. You figured out a way, not only to get control of

Spearhead by having Valentine marry her, but to make quick money by starting a fake land rush. You destroyed Buck Carmody's real will and forged one to suit yourself. That was only one of other forgeries. Then you started the story that Mid C was going to build by way of Spearhead and that Tamarack would be abandoned. You've been buying back land here in town for a cent on the dollar, knowing it will boom again when the truth comes out."

"A pack of lies!" Owen shouted.

Jim Hennessy spoke: "We figure that Josh Enright threatened to expose you as a skin game artist. So you waited for him at the Moccasin Crick ford when he was on his way back to E Loop after talking to you here in town . . . just like you waited a few minutes ago for his son. Valentine was with you at that time. You shot Josh Enright while he was talking to you."

"You can't prove any of these ridiculous charges," Owen said, but now there was an uncertainty in him.

"There are one or two other things we haven't got clear in our minds, Owen," Bell said. "One is that mortgage you hold on E Loop. I figure that's a forgery, too. Just how you got it recorded and back-dated we don't know. Likely you bribed somebody in the county office. That will be easy to uncover."

"We'll talk it over at your office, Owen," Jim Hennessy said. "Maybe you can think of some reason why you shouldn't be hung for what you've done."

They left by way of the kitchen and followed the same circuitous path Bell had used in order to avoid attention. The two girls and Teresa Drake refused to be left out. Nancy laid a hand on Bell's arm, and Alice and her mother walked with Irons as they followed the sheriff and his prisoner.

Finally they stood at the rear door of Owen's private office. Hennessy searched Owen and found a key that admitted them. "What now?" Owen demanded surlily.

"We'll wait!" Bell said. He motioned to the others and they filed into the larger adjoining office and arranged themselves where they would not be visible through the intervening open door that was left open.

"What are we waiting for?" Owen demanded.

"It's a good place," Bell said. "Quiet. Peaceful. I haven't had much of that lately."

"You're making a fool's mistake!" Owen raged.

"You're the one who made the mistakes, Owen. One was when you overlooked the fact there was a witness in the brush at Moccasin Ford when you shot Josh. You didn't know that until I showed you Matt Barker's letter. Another mistake was when you fired that shot through the window of Nancy Carmody's room at the Mountain House. Before that, you had used that same Thirty-Eight for target practice to while away time when you made a trip into the Pouch to make sure Josh had been telling the truth about the place. I found the empty shells. That linked you with everything that had happened. I had first begun to suspect you at the time those guns opened up on Barker and me at Sid Durkin's house. But all I could do was run like a rabbit with a broken leg."

Irons spoke again. "There's a little more to it. Owen made sure that the story of the outlaw days of Josh Enright was kept alive so there'd be no real sympathy for Bell, no matter what happened to him." He turned to Nancy. "An' he an' Valentine an' Murdock also kept paintin' you as a wild one. He didn't want anyone to stand up for you, no matter how peculiar that marriage provision in the fake will might stack up. So he circulated lies about you. He made you out as a very fast woman."

"A scarlet one," Nancy said. "I wonder if I'll ever be able to live it down?"

"It would be just terribly fascinating to try," Alice said.

"Imagine! A woman with a past, even though it was only manufactured out of whole cloth!"

"You're arresting the wrong man, Hennessy!" Owen croaked. "Enright helped this man, Barker, escape from jail and helped in the murder of your turnkey."

"On the contrary, I've got witnesses who say Bell's pistol could not have been fired more than a few times and that was in self-defense," Hennessy said. "As for helping in a jail break, Matt Barker was still in Durkin's custody when he was killed. In addition, there were mitigating circumstances. No crime was committed, in my opinion, and . . . ."

Bell made a warning gesture for silence, and everyone in the room quit breathing for a moment. They heard sounds in the outer alleyway. Then fingernails raked the door panel.

Bell arose silently, moved to the wall, and stood so that he could not be seen. Then he turned the knob on the night lock and let the door swing open.

Only Owen, sitting at the desk, was in view through the portal, and a man stepped across the threshold and started to say: "Owen, we just got into town and . . . ."

It was Leach Valentine. At his heels strode Shep Murdock. Then Valentine became aware something was wrong. He whirled and saw Bell. At the same moment Irons stepped into the room through the opposite door.

"Kill them, Leach!" Owen shouted.

"Stand, Leach!" Bell warned. "Don't try it!" He had in his hand the six-shooter he had wrested from Valentine earlier in the day, and it was now back in working condition.

Valentine evidently had possessed another six-shooter, for he was carrying one in a holster. His hand had darted toward it, but now he halted, not wanting to force such an issue.

Murdock, however, with Valentine's bulk shielding him, drew and fired, feeling that he was reasonably safe. He shot at Irons, but Bell, sensing his intention, sent the door whizzing against Valentine an instant earlier. Valentine was pushed back a step and that was enough to deflect Murdock's gun. The bullet crashed into the wall to Irons's right.

That saved Irons, but it also imposed the door as a barrier between them and their quarry. Valentine and Murdock took instant advantage and raced away down the dark lane.

Bell charged through the doorway in pursuit, with Irons a stride behind him. Jim Hennessy was bawling: "Wait! This is a matter for the law!"

Guns flamed ahead and Bell heard the passage of bullets close by him. He fired twice in savage retaliation. Another slug plucked at the collar of his coat. He realized that he stood against a lighted background, for the alley was open at both ends and faint moonlight framed the entrances from either street.

He flattened against a wall, and Irons followed his example a few yards away. Valentine and Murdock also were hugging shadows.

Thus, for the space of twenty heartbeats there was utter silence and a deadlock. Any of the four who made a mistake might die, and they all knew it.

Bell broke the impasse. He went racing ahead four strides, then plunged to the ground in time to avoid the bullets both opponents hurled in his direction. He arose as the gun roar ceased and made another foray, and now Irons began shooting down the alley to cover his advance.

A six-shooter exploded so close Bell felt the heat of the blast, and he fired hip high from a crouching position. He heard a sound as of cloth being ripped. A man uttered a long, wheezing gasp and moaned entreatingly: "No . . . ."

It was Shep Murdock. Bell stumbled over his slumped body. Irons's gun roared almost at his side. Then Valentine began shouting in a thin, eerie voice: "Don't shoot any more! I've thrown down my gun!"

"Stand out there where we can see you," Irons commanded. "An' will you talk?"

"I'll talk," Valentine panted.

Jim Hennessy came at a heavy-footed run and snapped handcuffs on the man. Other citizens arrived, and someone brought a lantern. Shep Murdock was alive, but with a bullet in him. Dr. Ulysses Sylvester ordered him taken to his office and ventured the opinion that he would live.

"To be hanged," the sheriff stated.

They led Valentine into the office where Owen Randolph sat. Valentine was shaking now, and talking hysterically, and answering all the questions that were put to him. He was willing to tell everything in the hope of winning clemency

"You weakling!" Owen frothed. "You're only talking both of us into a noose."

Valentine corroborated what Bell and the others had already pieced together from circumstantial evidence—even to the forging of Buck Carmody's will and the forgery of the encumbrance that had been filed against E Loop.

Bell turned away. Nancy stood with Alice and Mrs. Drake in the background. He walked toward her, and she suddenly straightened and a soft, shy radiance came upon her, for she had become aware of his purpose.

Alice laughed, kissed her, and said: "You've known this for days, and so has he. Bell and I never were in love the way you and he are in love. We'd never have married."

Bell took Nancy in his arms and kissed her slowly, wonderingly at first, and then with a fierce ardor. Even now he expected her to draw away and show him that neutrality he had come to expect from her. But her mouth clung to his own with a wild and warm abandon while her arms held him ever tighter.

Presently she drew back, her gray eyes filled with high laughter. "Darling," she murmured. "We have a whole lifetime ahead. Just think of it."

Then, her arm on his, they walked together from Owen Randolph's office. Main Street was crowded. The saloons had emptied and their patrons lined the sidewalks to stare. The word had reached the knockdown dance halls and gambling houses on Front Street, and these had spewed forth customers, gamblers, and entertainers. Percentage girls in spangles, and grifters and shell-game artists and short-card sports came to gaze. And there were Irish section hands, horny-fisted graders and tampers, for two full trains had just pulled in, bringing construction men and material. Along with them had come Henry Driscoll in his private car to announce that end of steel was going to move westward.

Side-by-side, Bell and Nancy walked through these people and on down the street and into the Mountain House. Now he saw that Irons, with Alice on his arm, was following closely behind them.

The plump and many-petticoated Jenny Walking Elk appeared, and went hurrying up the stairs ahead of them. And old Wilcey Pickens brought up the rear, his feathered features alight. He was the last of the Wild Bunch.

Now Bell picked up Nancy in his arms and walked down the hall toward the sitting room suite she had occupied the day they had first talked. Jenny Walking Elk, beaming like a great bronze moon, threw open the door with a flourish and beckoned them to enter. "You his real squaw soon!" she crackled at Nancy. "You ketch him for sure."

In the room he sat Nancy down. "Somebody fetch a preacher," he said.

"But we're already married," Nancy said, and a great happiness was swelling within her.

Irons spoke. "I'll see to it that the preacher's time isn't wasted." Then he looked at Alice and added: "That's a proposal."

She moved to him and kissed him lustily and completely. "That," she said, blushing furiously, "is an acceptance!" Then Alice added, with something of her former primness: "But there'll be no wedding tonight. Not in this outfit. Breeches and boots. *Ugh!* I want something silky and soft. Something old and something . . . something bold."

She kissed Irons again, then embraced Nancy and Bell. Afterward, she wept tears of joy and Nancy joined her.

Jenny Walking Elk, still cackling shrilly, forced both Bell and Irons out of the room. "Both come back tomorrow," she ordered. "No see-um squaws no more tonight. Bad luck before wedding."

"We *are* married!" Bell protested.

Jenny glared uncompromisingly. "First one not for keeps," she declared. "You marry her again . . . for real. I be there. I make sure. Me, Jenny Walking Elk."

Bell and Irons went down the stairs, arm in arm. On the sidewalk they looked up.

Nancy and Alice were at a window, blowing kisses to them. Then Jenny Walking Elk snatched the girls away, and closed the window.

They stood listening to the laughter that came faintly from the room. No longer were there any tears.

ABOUT THE AUTHOR

Cliff Farrell was born in Zanesville, Ohio, where earlier Zane Grey had been born. Following graduation from high school, Farrell became a newspaper reporter. Over the next decade he worked his way west by means of a string of newspaper jobs and for thirty-one years was employed, mostly as sports editor, for the *Los Angeles Examiner*. He would later claim that he began writing for pulp magazines because he grew bored with journalism. His first Western stories were written for *Cowboy Stories* in 1926 and his byline was A. Clifford Farrell. By 1928 this byline was abbreviated to Cliff Farrell, and this it remained for the rest of his career. In 1933 Farrell was invited to contribute a story for the first issue of *Dime Western*. He soon became a regular contributor to this magazine and to *Star Western* as well. In fact, many months he would have a short novel in both magazines. Farrell became such a staple at Popular Publications that by the end of the 1930s he was contributing as much as 400,000 words a year to their various Western magazines. In all, Farrell wrote nearly 600 stories for the magazine market. His earliest Western fiction tended to stress action and gun play, but increasingly his stories began to focus on characters in historical situations and the problems faced by those characters. *Follow The New Grass* (1954) was Farrell's first Western novel, a story concerned with a desperate battle over grazing rights in the Cheyenne Indian reserve. It was followed by *West With The Missouri* (1955), an exciting story of riverboats, gamblers, and gunmen. *Fort Deception* (1960), *Ride The Wild Country* (1963), *The Renegade* (1970), and *The Devil's Playground* (1976) are among the best of Farrell's later Western novels. *Desperate Journey* (Five Star Westerns, 1999), a first collection of Cliff Farrell's Western short stories, has appeared, and more recently *The White Feather* (Five Star Westerns, 2004).